"Why Did You Come Here Tonight, Harris?" Sarah Asked Warily

"For this...." he answered, lowering his head and taking her mouth with his.

Damn. Sarah knew she'd been dancing around the fire since the moment she met this man. If the flames were only coming from her, she could have resisted. But she'd seen something in Harris that called to her soul. Something that said he'd been wounded as often as she had. Something that said she could heal him.

And yet, even as the kiss deepened, he revealed no emotion at all. That made her want to force a reaction from him. She sensed the passion seething beneath the surface, and she wanted to unleash it.

But now she wondered if she'd be releasing more than she could handle....

Dear Reader,

Welcome to another stellar month of stories from Silhouette Desire. We kick things off with our DYNASTIES: THE BARONES series as Kristi Gold brings us *Expecting the Sheikh's Baby* in which—yes, you guessed it!—a certain long-lost Barone cousin finds herself expecting a very special delivery.

Also this month: The fabulous Peggy Moreland launches a brand-new series with THE TANNERS OF TEXAS, about *Five Brothers and a Baby,* which will give you the giddy-up you've been craving. The wonderful Brenda Jackson is back with another story about her Westmoreland family. *A Little Dare* is full of many big surprises…including a wonderful secret-child story line. And *Sleeping with the Boss* by Maureen Child will have you on the edge of your seat—or boardroom table, whatever the case may be.

KING OF HEARTS, a new miniseries by Katherine Garbera, launches with *In Bed with Beauty*. The series focuses on an angel with some crooked wings who must do a lot of matchmaking in order to secure his entrance through the pearly gates. And Laura Wright is back with *Ruling Passions,* a very sensual royal-themed tale.

So, get ready for some scintillating storytelling as you settle in for six wonderful novels. And next month, watch for Diana Palmer's *Man in Control*.

More passion to you!

Melissa Jeglinski

Melissa Jeglinski
Senior Editor, Silhouette Desire

Please address questions and book requests to:
Silhouette Reader Service
U.S.: 3010 Walden Ave., P.O. Box 1325, Buffalo, NY 14269
Canadian: P.O. Box 609, Fort Erie, Ont. L2A 5X3

In Bed with
Beauty
KATHERINE GARBERA

Published by Silhouette Books

America's Publisher of Contemporary Romance

For those who went before me and left behind the wonderful stories
of another time. My great-uncle Tony Festa, great-aunt Dorothy Festa,
great-uncle Gennaro "Sonny" Tedesco
and my grandmother Rose Tedesco Wilkinson.

Acknowledgments:

Thanks to Mary Louise Wells who knows everything
and always has an answer when I call her with one of my questions.

Thanks as always to Matt, Courtney and Lucas for all the love and support.

SILHOUETTE BOOKS

ISBN 0-373-76535-5

IN BED WITH BEAUTY

Copyright © 2003 by Katherine Garbera

This edition published by arrangement with Harlequin Books S.A.

® and TM are trademarks of Harlequin Books S.A., used under license.
Trademarks indicated with ® are registered in the United States Patent
and Trademark Office, the Canadian Trade Marks Office and in other
countries.

Visit Silhouette at www.eHarlequin.com

Printed in U.S.A.

Books by Katherine Garbera

Silhouette Desire

The Bachelor Next Door #1104
Miranda's Outlaw #1169
Her Baby's Father #1289
Overnight Cinderella #1348
Baby at His Door #1367
Some Kind of Incredible #1395
The Tycoon's Temptation #1414
The Tycoon's Lady #1464
Cinderella's Convenient Husband #1466
Tycoon for Auction #1504
Cinderella's Millionaire #1520
*In Bed with Beauty #1535

*King of Hearts

KATHERINE GARBERA

spends her days writing and creating stories in which there are always happy endings. She believes in these troubled times that we need more focus on all that is good and right in our world. She is happily married to the man she met in Fantasyland and lives in Florida with him and their two children. You can visit her on the Web at katherinegarbera.com.

AUTHOR'S NOTE

Il Re is a stylized mob *Capo*. Many Italian-Americans aren't fond of the Mafia depictions used in the media and that isn't the focus of this character. Il Re is an unfortunate fellow who got lucky. He wasn't a good guy in his time on earth, but he is finding salvation in his new role of matchmaker.

Because of the nature of series romance, the kind of realistic language used by mobsters isn't acceptable. I had to find something to substitute for all those creative uses of the F-word. I decided to used some Italian terms.

Italian terms Il Re uses and their meanings:

Madon':	(sometimes spelled *Maddon'*) short for Madonna, meaning holy smoke, holy cow.
babbeo	a dope, idiot, useless underling
Capo:	the Family member who leads a crew
compare:	crony, close pal, buddy
agita:	anxiety, edginess, an upset stomach

Prologue

"**P**asquale Mandetti, an opportunity stands before you." The female voice was soft and sultry, taking me by surprise. No one called me by my given name.

"That's Il Re to you, babe." I stared up into the blinding light. Holy Cow, could I still be alive? Nah, no one lives through being shot five times in the chest with a Glock.

"In the afterworld there is only one King."

I shrugged. I wasn't going to argue with God or God's emissary. "Then call me Ray."

"There is a chance for you to redeem yourself, Ray."

I laughed. This broad was too much! "Me? Yeah, right. A guy like me doesn't just play nice once he's dead and still manage to get to heaven."

"With your dying breath you asked for forgiveness. He likes to do what he can."

All right. "Great, so I'm going Up?"

"Not so fast. There are conditions."

Of course there were. *Madon'* I was acting like a *babbeo.* There was no such thing as a free ride. "I'm listening."

"We want you to unite in love as many couples as enemies you murdered in hate on earth."

"Hell—"

"We don't use that term here."

"Excuse me," I said sarcastically. "I was a *capo* for twenty-five years, I ordered a lot of men killed. And that doesn't count the scuffles I had making it to the top."

"We know you were a crime boss. We don't have all day. Will you be accepting this offer?"

"Babe, I thought we had eternity."

"You don't have a prayer if you call me babe again."

I bit back a chuckle. This broad was feisty. "Okay, I'll do it."

"There are a few rules."

I spread my hands. Hey, I could do a few jobs. It wouldn't be the first time. "I'm not exactly a rule-abiding kinda guy."

"You're about to experience a modification," she said. "First, you will select a couple for the assignment. You will take on human form and a new persona each time. Once the couple is together I will appear to you again."

"That's all?" *Piece of cake.* Heaven here I come.

"Not quite. If they don't fall in love on their own, you have to help them."

What did I know about love? I knew what it took to destroy a relationship, but I'd never been able to hold onto a woman. Even the ones who weren't looking for forever had deserted me long before I was ready to let them go. *Merda,* this wasn't going to be easy. "What, do I look like a marriage counselor?"

"You better hope you do to them."

An image of Tess, the only woman who'd ever tried to make my life better, who'd loved me through things that would have destroyed a lesser woman, swam in front of my face. It wasn't a happy image, I'd done what I could to destroy the feelings she'd brought to life in me. Did what I could to survive in a world where a soft man—a man in love couldn't survive.

But this world was different. I'd do it for Tess. In repayment of the love she'd given me. The love I'd never taken the time to realize I wanted until it had been too late. "So, who's up first?"

A stack of manila file folders appeared on her desk. "Pick a number."

"Cute. Just give me one." I definitely didn't like this broad.

"Number one. Good place to start," she said.

She held the file folder toward me. I flipped it open and scanned the file. Sarah Malcolm, a struggling restaurant owner and Harris Davidson, a wealthy CEO. They had nothing in common. Skimming farther down the didn't page help. These two weren't meant for each other.

"You've got to be kidding me. No way in he—heck, these two are going to fall in love. Give me another one."

The pile disappeared. "The system doesn't work that way. It's your job to see that they fall in love. And the Boss likes them married," she said, standing up and walking to the front of the desk.

"If I fail?" She had nice legs. It didn't change the fact that she pissed me off, but I filed that tidbit away for later consideration.

"You asked Him for forgiveness," she reminded me.

"Yeah, but I never thought I'd get it."

"Well, you did. Do you have any other questions?" she asked.

A million questions. This was the strangest thing I'd ever experienced. But I couldn't screw up. Matchmaker, damn if my *compares* saw me now they'd be laughing their asses off. "Yeah, how do I contact you?"

"I'll be around."

She disappeared in a puff of smoke. What a comedown, I thought, as my body began to fade. Once a *capo* in the mob and now freakin' matchmaker to the lovelorn. Holy Mary, what a mess.

One

Sarah Malcolm was late. This was nothing new. She'd tried all the techniques for timeliness out there. Setting the clock ahead fifteen minutes, mapping out alternate timesaving routes, wearing two watches. Still, she was never on time.

Today she'd enlisted the twins' help to be out of the house in a timely fashion and they'd made sure she was. Unfortunately she hadn't planned on her car breaking down. It seemed a little juvenile to kick the tire of her late-model sedan so she waited until the oncoming cars passed her before she did it. Just once she wanted everything to go her way.

Citrus Grove Bank was her last chance at keeping her restaurant, Taste of Home open. And if she was late, she was pretty sure, Mr. Max Tucker wouldn't be impressed by her abilities to run a tight ship. Tucker wouldn't give money to someone who couldn't even be on time.

Damn.

This was the end. She'd have to give up the business, and take two jobs just to support herself and her siblings, eighteen-year-old twins. On the plus side the twins would be leaving for college next September and they did have full scholarships. But that was almost a year for her to keep things together. To give them the home her parents had wanted for them.

The beginnings of a headache started at the base of her neck. She wished she'd checked in with the Magic 8 ball this morning before leaving. But there hadn't been time. She might have checked her horoscope as well but she'd had to cancel her newspaper subscription.

A limousine coasted to a stop right in front of her. Sarah blinked; sure she was imagining it. A short, slightly rotund man emerged from the front. He wore a pair of casual pants, a dress shirt and a tie with, of all things, angels on it.

It looked out of character on the balding man. His shirt stretched tight across his belly. He had an olive complexion and beard stubble despite the early hour. He stopped in front of her car.

"Hey, babe. Flat tire?" he asked, with a Jersey accent.

"I wish." He made her smile with his self-assured grin and easy manner.

The back door to the limo opened and a second

man emerged. He was tall with blond hair, and he moved toward them with a purpose. His eyes were a bright gray that cut right through her. She knew by looking at him that this second man commanded power. His clothing was straight from *GQ,* from his hand-sewn Italian shoes to his designer suit.

As he came closer, she sucked in her breath. His features were too sharp to be termed handsome but he was attractive. She wished she hadn't learned long ago that there was no such thing as fairy tales because he looked a lot like her version of Prince Charming. But she'd dated enough frogs to know that P.C. didn't exist except in childhood dreams. And it had been a long time since Sarah Malcolm had been a child.

"What's the problem?" he asked. He wore a striped shirt underneath his navy suit. His tie was dark. She smiled as he moved closer to her, realizing his tie had small sharks, swimming with their jaws open on it.

"I don't know," she said.

He glanced at his watch then at his limo driver. "Can we drop you somewhere?"

What a gentleman, she thought. It seemed like all those candles she'd been lighting at church had finally paid off. She'd been praying for a man to come into her life.

"That would be great. I've called a tow truck but it won't be here for a half hour. I'm due at the Citrus Grove Bank over on Kaley in fifteen minutes."

"Then let's get going," he said, pivoting to walk back to the car.

Sarah hesitated. She wasn't sure she should just hop into a limousine with two strange men. True, she'd been praying for a handsome knight to rescue her. But she'd been doing that since she'd turned eighteen and Paul had decided two six-year-old twins wasn't what he wanted from life. So far the guys who'd come along hadn't been that splendid.

"On second thought I think I'll wait for the tow."

The chauffeur stopped and looked straight at her. There was something in his eyes that reassured her. But then she'd heard Ted Bundy had nice eyes.

"Look, it's no problem. I'm bonded," he said. He pulled a card from his back pocket and handed it to her. Bella Notte Limousine Services. The card had a state certification number as well as the driver's name—Ray King.

"Thanks." She glanced at the man who disturbed her on a deep emotional level. He walked back toward her, stopping a discreet distance away.

"Harris Davidson," he said, sticking out his hand.

"Sarah Malcolm." She took his hand, pumped it three times and let it drop. But her palm still tingled from the contact. His nails were manicured, but she was sure she felt calluses on his hands. She filed the incongruity away for later.

"Now that we're old friends, can we please go?" he asked.

Was that sarcasm in his voice? She wasn't sure, so she smiled up at him the way she did at her accountant when he gave her news she didn't like.

"Sure. Thanks for giving me ride," she said to Harris.

Sarah slid into the car, taking a seat on the far bench. The divider was up between the driver's area and the back. She wondered if the driver had made the decision to stop on his own.

Harris was seated and soon they were moving down Orange Avenue. Orlando was a pretty city especially in early fall. The dog days of summer had ended and Halloween was around the corner. She'd already started decorating her house.

"Thanks for stopping."

"You're welcome," he said.

She realized he wasn't going to talk to her again until they got to the bank. That was fine. She could respect his wishes. She glanced at her watch, whispered a fervent prayer that time would slow down a little and she wouldn't be late.

What would her mom do in this situation? Sarah honestly didn't know. She'd always tried to be as different from her parents as she could. So filling their shoes had been doubly hard for her.

She couldn't stand her own thoughts any longer.

"Do you live around here?" she asked. She hated silence, particularly with strangers. Nervous chatter was one of her faults. Her brother teasingly called her Mouth-of-the-South because of it.

"No. California," he said.

She sank back into the leather seat, crossing her legs. His eyes tracked the movement. She tugged at the hem of her skirt.

She had really fat knees. It didn't matter that she could wear a size six, her knees always looked to her like they belonged on an elephant and his gaze made her self-conscious.

"Where? San Diego, Los Angeles or San Francisco?" she asked.

He finally looked away, clearing his throat. "L.A.—Belair actually."

"Really?"

He inclined his head and lifted one eyebrow. He had a tendency to react with an acerbic wit, she realized, even when he didn't speak.

She knew he wanted her to leave him alone, but there was something about him. The aloofness he portrayed made her want to needle him. To keep talking until he had no choice but to respond to her.

"Do you know any movie stars? I've always wanted to visit, but I've never had the chance."

"I don't know any movie stars," he said, picking up the Wall Street Journal from the seat next to him, snapping it open.

She knew it was a hint. A pretty blatant one considering he lifted the paper until she couldn't see his face. She glanced out the window; they were coming closer to the bank. Any minute now, she'd be placing the restaurant's fate in Mr. Tucker's hands. What if he denied her the expansion loan?

"Do you like living there?" she asked, needing to distract herself.

"I guess so," he said from behind the paper.

Sarah liked a challenge. She waited a few minutes. "Could you live anywhere else?"

He lowered a corner of the paper. "Not without relocating my business. I like L.A. I deal mostly with the Asian market."

"What do you do?"

"Ms. Malcolm—"

"Call me Sarah," she said with a smile.

He set the paper on the seat next to him and leaned forward, arms braced against his knees. His jacket fell open and she noticed the muscles under his dress shirt as the fabric stretched tautly across his chest.

She wondered what he'd look like without his shirt on. Okay, she'd definitely been alone too long. Time to start dating again. In fact, when she got back to the restaurant she'd call Marcus, her accountant, and take him up on his standing invitation for dinner.

"Do I make you nervous?" he asked.

His question startled her. Did she seem nervous? "No, why?"

"Do you always talk so much?"

"I'm afraid so. My brother teases me mercilessly about it."

"I'm not your brother," he said.

"Believe me, I noticed," she said before she could stop herself.

He cocked his head to the side, watching her with an intensity that made her acutely aware of her femininity.

The limo stopped in front of the bank and Sarah

gathered her stuff to get out. Harris stopped her with a hand on her arm. "Don't go quiet on me now."

"I thought that was your fondest wish."

"Maybe you don't know everything."

"There's no maybe about it."

"I like a woman who's not afraid to admit she doesn't know everything."

"Most men do. It makes them feel superior," she said, with a wink.

Harris wasn't sure how to reply to Sarah. No one ever really teased him the way she had. He worked hard to keep a wall between himself and others. He wasn't positive, but he thought she might have realized that and then decided to do her damnedest to break through it. He'd held his own against some of the shrewdest Japanese investors at the bargaining table but this one rather slight woman knocked him off balance.

"In the battle of the sexes, men will take any advantage."

She smiled, drawing his attention to her mouth. She had the sexiest damn mouth he'd ever seen. Her lips were full, but not so they looked like they were about to explode. Instead they beckoned a man closer. Teased him into believing that one taste from her lips would be as close to nirvana as he might find on this earth.

"Even a false one," she said.

Hell, what had they been talking about? Women had an advantage over men, they'd never really understand, Harris thought. Because when a man was with a woman he'd just met and he hadn't ruled her out as lover, only that thought dominated him. "A perceived advantage can't hurt."

She tossed her hair. It was thick and black, kind of curly. It looked free and untamed much as her spirit had said she was. There was a rich shine to it and he knew it would feel like sable under his fingers.

It had been a long time since he'd taken a mistress. He wondered if she'd be open to that type of arrangement. He'd only be in Orlando for six weeks. The situation would be ideal for him.

"Just as long as you know it's only perceived," she said. Her voice was mellow, deeper than most women's were. A soft alto that brushed over his senses like a silk brush over his skin. Awakening a part of him that he'd thought dormant.

If there was one thing Harris knew it was that the deck was stacked against men in the battle of the sexes. He'd watched his own father fall victim one too many times to the supposed weaker sex to ever allow himself to be that weak. In his twenties he'd ignored the lessons he'd learned at his father's knee and tried to create the family he'd always craved. He'd failed and never attempted it again. "Believe me I do."

"Bitter?" she asked.

He thought about it. He held no ill will toward womankind, had enjoyed many a night in a woman's arms. But there was clearly a battlefield when it came to the two genders. Men, or at least Harris, felt ill equipped for the battle.

"Just realistic."

"Oh, *realistic*. Are you one of those guys who doesn't believe in love?" she asked.

She leaned forward on the seat, her dark brown eyes sparkled. Suddenly he wanted to do something juvenile like challenge her to a dare. She was the kind of woman who'd relish it.

She wasn't like other women he'd met before. She sparkled with a *joie de vie* that he'd never had, and the selfish, cold part of him wanted to keep her close so that he could bask in her warmth. But he knew she wouldn't stay for long. Then again, she didn't have to, he reminded himself. He only wanted her for the length of his stay in Florida.

Many women had tried to change him. Tried to teach him to love, but Harris knew some things came into a man's life too late. And love was certainly one of those things for him.

"Honey, no man believes in love," he said.

Her eyes shuttered and he realized she'd categorized him. *Genus Male, Species Hopeless.*

"Just lust, huh?" she asked.

"Well lust is quantitatively provable," he said. He needed to touch her again. Earlier when they'd shook hands he'd been preoccupied with getting back on the road so he wouldn't be late for his appointment. But now he wanted to linger. That reaction shook him. He wasn't given to unpredictable actions and didn't intend to start now.

"You have a point," she said.

"I usually do."

She gathered her purse, dug inside it for her sunglasses. "What about relationships that last after physical desire fades?"

He saw Ray moving around to open the door. Harris wasn't too sure about this new driver. His normal one, Jeffrey O'Neil, wasn't available due to a family emergency and it seemed Ray King didn't really understand his role. Harris had learned early on that staff wasn't family and should be treated like employees. He would remind Ray of this as soon as they dropped Sarah Malcolm off. He'd learned early on that roles were important and to make sure everyone understood the part they were to play.

Part of him saddened that this encounter was going to end so soon. "What about them?"

"Why do they continue?" she asked.

Honestly, he'd never had one last after the intense passion faded. He didn't know why they did. He'd noticed that some of the woman he'd dated had tried to strike up a friendship with him after some time had passed. But Harris knew that relationships of any kind weren't for him. He was more comfortable with the silence. "Friendship, I guess," he said.

"That's all."

"I've never experienced one, but I'd guess a long-term monogamous relationship lasts because of the memories of hot sex and the bond of friendship."

"You really are a guy," she said at last.

"Did I try to convince you I wasn't?" he asked.

"No," she said, blushing.

"Should I prove to you I am?" He wanted her to

say yes. But he'd never blow off his meeting for the chance to spend the day with her. No matter how much he wanted to explore the hot currents that burned between them. He slid forward in his seat so that their knees brushed.

She had great legs. It was one of the first things he'd noticed about her. Nicely rounded calves and smooth shins. Her legs were bare, her feet shod in backless sandals. There was a silver toe ring on her second toe.

"Why are you suddenly so talkative?" she asked, tugging at the hem of her skirt. He noticed earlier she'd done the same thing. This small vulnerability reassured him. She was self-conscious about her legs.

"Why are you suddenly so defensive?" he asked brushing her hands away from her knees as she reached again for the hem of her skirt. "The fabric isn't going to get longer."

Tugging her hands from under his, she glanced at the door. "Why hasn't he opened it?"

"Are you so anxious to escape?" he asked, finally he had the advantage with her and he wasn't ready to give it up.

She tucked a strand of hair behind her ear and then ran her hands down her torso, straightening the fabric of her floral print skirt. She looked like spring, he realized. "I don't want to be late for my appointment."

He consulted his watch. "You still have ten minutes."

"I...damn. You do make me nervous," she said at last.

Now we're getting somewhere he thought. Though she'd seemed different than other women, she wasn't really. He hadn't discovered her secrets, had barely scratched the surface but that comment made him realize he could find out what made her tick. "That's the last thing I want you to feel around me."

"Then stop looking at my legs."

The feisty woman was back. He liked the facets of Sarah. "I can't help it."

Ray opened the door. "Sorry about that. Someone asked for directions."

Harris nodded.

Sarah slid out of the car with a smooth motion, full of feminine grace. He liked her, more than he'd care to admit even to himself. But then Harris had been focused on business for too long. Maybe that explained the lust that had been riding him since she'd entered the car and he'd caught a glimpse of her backside.

Harris decided it was a good thing she was leaving now. He needed to regain his perspective and get back to business.

"Thanks for the ride," she said.

"You're welcome."

She bit her lower lip, then reached into her purse and pulled out a business card holder. "Here's my card. Drop by my restaurant anytime for a complimentary meal."

"That's not necessary," Harris said.

"It is to me. I don't like to be in anyone's debt."

She turned to Ray and handed him a card as well. "Please come by some time."

She didn't wait for an answer but just turned and walked away. They both watched her leave. Harris more disturbed than he'd been in a long time. She rocked him from his safe moorings and he knew only one thing for certain. No way was he going to her restaurant.

Two

————·————

Two days later, Sarah was still thinking about Harris. Taste of Home, Sarah's restaurant, was known for its charming warmth, good food and friendly staff. Still, she had trouble making ends meet.

Mr. Tucker, her banker, had denied her expansion loan. Rumor had it her strip mall had been sold and the new owners were tearing it down to build one of those newly popular outdoor malls. Honestly, who wanted to shop outdoors in Florida? It was hot or rainy most of the time.

On top of everything else she didn't need this problem. All her life she'd thought she wanted to be a wife and mother. Raising her siblings had been challenging but now that they were almost launched into the world, she realized there were other things she wanted for herself. The only problem was she had yet to figure out what those they were.

She had enough trouble with the restaurant's financial state to keep her occupied, but that didn't stop her mind from wandering to Harris.

Situated a block from International Drive in the heart of Orlando's theme park district, her restaurant had a hard time competing with the big chains. Locals didn't want to fight the tourist traffic and tourists were reluctant to give her a try. Though lately, the concierge desks of several hotels were recommending her restaurant to their guests. She'd been schmoozing the hotel employees with free meals and it was paying off.

Tonight's crowd had been light but steady. Not bad considering that October wasn't exactly a booming month in the tourist industry. Sarah should have been jubilant, but instead she couldn't help but wonder why Harris Davidson hadn't come in for his free meal.

She reminded herself she was much to busy for a man in her life but that didn't seem to matter. She liked Harris. He made her feel like a woman.

She was seated in the back of the restaurant behind the kitchen in her office. It was a small room that had at one time served as a storage closet. She'd been unable to use the more spacious office that had been her dad's. Instead she and her siblings had decided to keep the office as it was when he died. It sounded strange but sometimes when she went in there she felt her parents presence. She could hear the culinary staff from her office and the sounds of cooking had always soothed her.

Sometimes when she was most frustrated with her life she'd spend hours in the kitchen baking. Baking was what she liked to do best, but her parents' dream had been a small homey restaurant, not a bakery.

Her desk fit from wall to wall against the back and her chair was a battered secretary model that she'd rescued from the dump. Lhasa, the Mexican vocalist, sang quietly in the background.

Sarah knew enough Spanish to know the singer sang of the heartache of love. Perhaps it wasn't her high school Spanish helping her out but her gut. Heartbreak sounded the same in every language.

That was part of her problem. Her entire life she'd been dreaming of finding true love and her instincts had always guided her to men who weren't interested in anything close to love. Although Paul had been close to love, he'd wanted his own family and not a ready-made one.

Reaching for the Magic 8 ball on her desk she shook it idly. It's not like she believed the 8 ball had special powers to see the future. It was just sometimes reassuring when she was uncertain.

She should've been relieved that Harris hadn't shown up at the restaurant. She should've been happy to know that the guy who was not even vaguely close to her Mr. Right didn't stop in. She should've been, but she wasn't.

"Will I see Harris again?" she asked and then

shook the black ball. Oh, God, if her brother saw her doing this he'd be laughing for a week.

Signs point to yes.

"Well where the heck is he?" she asked her empty office.

"Who?" said a voice from the doorway.

Sarah screamed and jumped out of her chair, pivoting to face Harris who stood in her office doorway. Damn, had she conjured him up by thinking about him?

"You gave me a heart attack," she said, holding her hand over her heart.

"My apologies," he said. But there was a sparkle in his eye that said he'd enjoyed startling her.

"What are you doing back here?" she asked.

"Your brother sent me back here when I asked to see you."

"Oh, you could have just given my card to your server and told them I comped your meal."

He walked into the room, stopping when only an inch of space remained between them. She knew it was ridiculous but she imagined she could feel his heat. He smelled of expensive cologne and was dressed again in a nice suit. She wasn't sure of the designer.

"I'm not here for a free meal," he said, his voice low.

She tilted her head back. A faint five-o'clock shadow dotted his chin and she wanted to touch his face. To feel the square jaw and roughness of the stubble darkening his face. She clenched her hands to keep from giving into the impulse.

"You're not?" she asked.

He shook his head. The song switched on her CD to Amado Mio and Sarah knew she should have hit stop as soon as he entered. Listening to Spanish love songs with this man around her wasn't a good idea.

"Why are you here?" Sarah asked.

He drew the tip of one finger down the curve of her cheek. She shuddered deep inside. His touch was light and gentle but started a riot in her senses. Deep inside the part of her that had been dormant for years woke. Not a gentle waking, it sprang abruptly to life.

"Why do you think?"

She couldn't imagine. Contemplating Harris was something she'd given up when his finger touched her face. His hand rested against her collarbone, his touch resting on her pulse. Which she knew was beating to fast for him not to notice.

"Oh, I don't want to guess."

"Come on, Sarah, meet me halfway," he said.

"It sounds like you want me to give your ego a boost," she said, stepping back. She needed to re- member this was a guy who at best would be looking for a vacation fling with her. She'd always been con- fident of herself and her worth. She wasn't going to forget it now.

"Ego has nothing to do with it."

She took his measure. He wanted something from her. She knew he'd spend the night in her bed if she offered but she needed more than just the physical from him. She'd always needed more which was probably why she'd been celibate for the better part of twelve years.

"You're the kind of woman who leaves a man guessing," he said after a few minutes. The music seemed too loud in her office. "You're like quicksilver, bright and flashing, but I know I can't hold you."

She'd never been called quicksilver before. And it touched her that he'd thought about holding her. His voice told her that he was about more than lust. "Do you want to?"

"Of course I do. I've been cold for a long time, Sarah and you're the promise of warmth."

"What kind of warmth?" she asked.

"Physical."

"I'm not like that," she said. Though she burned with the heat of desire, she needed more than that with any man.

"I know. That's why I stayed away."

"Why'd you come here tonight?" she asked at last. She wasn't sure what she'd expected from this businessman but him in her office wasn't it.

"Curiosity."

"About?" she asked.

"You."

This was too much. She needed some important answers before this went any further. She brushed past him and led the way out into the restaurant. She needed to be surrounded by people before she did something she'd regret. Something like fool herself that his disbelief in love didn't mean he never would care for any woman.

Ray was waiting in the main room when they reentered it. Obviously the talk Harris had with him yesterday about a driver's proper place meant nothing to the man. He'd have another discussion with him later and remind him that staff was supposed to stay in the background.

Sarah threw him off guard. He'd pursued women before and had a fair amount of success. Sarah was different. There was something about her that called to mind long-ago dreams. He pushed half-remembered memories away, refusing to dwell on those thoughts.

There was a small dance floor set off from the tables and the same music that had been playing in Sarah's office was piped in.

Ray quirked one eyebrow at him as their eyes met. That driver was too cocky by half, he thought.

Harris had a feeling he was going to be leaving here with some well-cooked food and that was all. He didn't want the hired help to know about it. He'd spent his entire life aware of the line that existed between himself and the people who were paid to serve him.

An older couple was on the dance floor moving slowly to the music. The restaurant had an old-world feeling of permanency and romance. Two things that he'd never felt comfortable with.

"Is our food ready?" Harris asked. It was time to cut his losses and get out while he still could.

"Not yet. Why don't you take Ms. Malcolm for a spin on the dance floor? I'll check on the food," Ray said.

"Do you dance?" Sarah asked.

Of course he did. Every Davidson was raised to socialize. But he didn't want to dance with her. Lust was riding him hard and there was something in her eyes that said he'd never get her in his bed. He needed to get out of this restaurant which brought to mind all the things he'd always wanted but could never have.

The music switched and Rosemary Clooney started singing "Mambo Italiano."

"How about a mambo?"

"Pardon me?" Harris asked. He'd come here tonight...hell, he didn't know why. He wanted her. But he wouldn't have acted on it...would he?

Yeah, right. He'd been trying to come up with an excuse to see her again. Finally, Ray had brought him here saying they had to eat. Ray had made him feel like he was hiding from a woman, which had bothered him. Harris was a man of action so when they'd arrived he'd sought out Sarah to prove something to himself.

All Harris had been able to think of was those long curvy legs of hers. He wasn't hungry for food at all. He had a bone-deep craving for her. She'd disturbed him the last couple of days. He'd been in meetings that were long and intense. His mind had wondered at the worst possible moments, as his kept coming back to Sarah.

"Dance?" she said, moving around him.

He followed her reluctantly. He and Ray had ordered their meals to go, at Harris' insistence. His plan had been simple. See Sarah, tease himself with her nearness and maybe if she were willing, kiss those sweet lips of hers. But he'd noticed the first time they met that logic flew out the window when Sarah Malcolm was in the room.

Her skirt swished around her knees as she walked. Her top was one of those little shirts, with barely any sleeves, that left her arms bare. She had nice arms with defined muscles. He wondered if her thighs were muscled as well. The skirt kicked up with each step she took but not enough for him to see.

"Ready?" she asked when they'd entered the main dining area. Burt, her brother, still manned the host stand.

"For what?" asked Burt. Harris liked Sarah's brother. Though obviously still a teenager he had an air of maturity seldom found in a boy his age.

"Mambo," Harris said.

"Oh, no. You should've said you don't dance in public," Burt said.

"Burt, hush. Harris wants to learn," Sarah said, swatting her brother on the arm.

"Sis, no man wants to learn how to mambo."

"If they want the ladies to love them they do."

Burt gave his sister a look that was pure-young-adult-male. "I'll settle for lust."

"Burt, that may be why you are working tonight instead of being out on date like Isabella."

Winking at Harris, he said, "Maybe I stayed home to help you out."

"We have staff," she reminded him.

Sarah was different around her sibling. And the difference told him he should back away right now. This wasn't a woman who would be interested in at best five weeks with a man who lived across the continent.

The pictures in her office of her family. The romantic music she'd been listening to and the caring in her eyes as she teased her brother. This was a woman who truly believed in the romance and fairy tale that was happily ever after.

"You want to learn, right?" she asked pinning her gaze on Harris.

He had a feeling this was test. Damn, he wished he'd stayed in the limo instead of giving into the impulse to see her again. He knew better than to follow his whims, they always led to trouble. "Uh…"

"Go on, Harris," Ray said.

"It's not that bad. The Millers are already out there and the other customers aren't paying any attention to the dance floor." Burt said.

"Let's go," Harris said.

He led Sarah to the dance floor and realized she was nervous. She chewed on her lower lip. Dammit. He wanted to taste her. To suckle that full lower lip with his mouth. He cared less about the mambo or humiliation. He wanted her in his arms. Once he had her there then he'd feel like he was in control again.

And nothing was more important to Harris Davidson than control. He took her in his arms and told
himself she didn't feel as if she'd been made for his
embrace. It was only physical compatibility. Nothing
more.

"Do you feel the same way Burt does?"

"About what?"

She pinned him with her gaze. For such wide
brown eyes they could be very intense. "Lust or
love?"

"Lust, remember?"

"The quantitative thing?"

"Yes."

"Let's see if one dance can change your mind,"
she said.

"It's going to take a hell of a lot more than the
mambo. I can tell you that."

"We'll see. I'll show you the steps of the dance.
You seem smart, so you should pick it up quickly."

"Glad to know I seem smart. I'd hate to think my
M.B.A. from Harvard was a fluke."

"Harvard?"

He nodded.

"I might have to rethink my position on your intelligence."

Sarah took one of his hands from her waist and
placed it on her hip. She moved the other one up to
her shoulder.

She showed him the movements of the dance. The
footwork was simple. And he intentionally flubbed it
a few times to feel her leg rub against his. Her legs

felt as good as he'd known they would. Her hips moved with each step and she watched him intently from under the long curls framing her face.

There was something so earnest about her that he had a moment's pause. Hurting women wasn't his thing. He'd never deceived anyone before and didn't intend to start now. This woman with her warm and friendly restaurant deserved better from him.

He'd recognized the property when they'd driven up. This was one of the locations the consortium was preparing to buy out. And he knew this group of men well enough to guess there'd be no place for Sarah's restaurant in their new complex. But that was business. And that was also why he couldn't get involved with Sarah. Too many complications.

A smattering of applause brought him back to where they where.

"One more time?" Burt asked.

Sarah shook her head. But never took her eyes off Harris's face. "I'll go check on your food."

Harris knew she was trying to get away from him. Knew he should let her go. But he followed her. The kitchen was busy. Harris took her hand and tugged her into her office instead.

"I didn't come here tonight for food," he said.

"You didn't?"

"No."

"Why did you come here?"

"For this," he said, lowering his head and taking her mouth with his.

Three

Damn. He smelled too good to resist. Sarah knew she'd been dancing around the fire, since the moment she first met Harris. If the flames were only coming from her she could resist it but she saw something in Harris that called to her soul. Something that said he'd been wounded as often as she had. Something that called to her heart and said she could heal him.

There was something in his frozen eyes that made her want to force a reaction from him. She wasn't surprised when he lowered his head toward hers. Or when his mouth moved on hers with subtlety, seducing her with gentle nibbling kisses that made her blood run heavy and brought all her nerve endings to life.

She sensed the passion seething beneath the surface

and had wanted to unleash it but now that she had—
she knew that she may have released more than she
could handle. She'd made love with men before but
they'd never made her feel a tenth what Harris was
making her feel with this one kiss.

He was a man who appreciated fine things. She'd
noticed that first about him. And he treated her in his
arms as if she were a living breathing work of art and
he wasn't letting go until he'd uncovered all her secrets.

She shuddered. She didn't want to be vulnerable to
him. He had defenses she wasn't sure she could ever
breach and she wasn't in the market for heartache.

But his touch left no room for doubt. No room for
thought even. The heat generated by the dancing and
being in his arms fanned the flame.

Harris wasn't a novice kisser. His mouth moved
expertly over hers. Nibbling at her lower lip before
sucking it into his mouth. She rose on tiptoe and tilted
her head to the left to better accommodate him.

He lifted his hands to support her neck as he thrust
his tongue deep inside her mouth. He tasted of breath
mints and something else. Something salty and masculine. Something she'd never tasted before but
wanted to again.

She slid her hands around his neck under his collar.
His skin was hot to her touch, and his pulse beat a
steady tattoo against his skin. Hers was beating just
a strongly. It gave her a sense of power to think she
affected him as deeply as he affected her.

It was only passion, she warned herself. But passion like she'd never experienced before. A wildfire out of control, she thought.

His hands slowly moved down her back, spanning her waist and pulling her more fully into his body. His chest was as hard as she'd suspected it would be. He pushed one of his thighs between her own. Her balance was no longer her own, but she didn't feel vulnerable in his arms. She felt completely safe and supported.

His mouth left hers as he dropped nibbling kisses down the length of her neck. "Tell me to stop now if you don't want more."

Sarah tried to think. She didn't know what she wanted. She couldn't find words to make him stop or urge him to continue. She took his jaw in her hands and stared up at him.

He ran one long finger down the side of her face. His touch stirring to life longings that she knew she shouldn't be feeling for him. Everything about him had warned her this wasn't a man who'd want more than her body. But her soul had been stirred from the first time they'd met.

She wanted to be the one to awaken the emotions she sensed he kept locked away. But she wasn't sure she was willing to pay the price.

She stepped back, taking his large hands in her own.

"I...oh, damn. This is more complicated than I thought it would be."

"Only if you make it complicated."

"What do you mean?" she asked.

"Come back to my hotel with me."

She wanted to. More than anything else it was what she wanted but life wasn't as simple as it had seemed just minutes earlier in his arms. And she'd never been able to sleep with a man and not let her emotions get involved.

"I need more time."

"I'm only in town for five more weeks."

That's it, she thought. Only five weeks. A keen disappointment filled her. "I'm sorry to hear that. But I can't add another complication to my life right now."

"You're a woman of honor. And there are damn few of those around."

"It's not honor that's driving me now," she said. She wanted Harris. But she wanted him for more than one night in her life.

"No?" he asked.

"I need more from you than just a few nights."

"That's all I have to offer," he said. "I like you Sarah, but I'm not going to change who I am."

"I'd just like to know you, not change you."

"You say that but at the core we're different people."

"Man and woman, I know."

"Not only that. You surround yourself with people you love—"

"And this is a bad thing?" she interrupted. Some guys didn't like women with family commitments. She knew that firsthand.

"It can be."

"Why?" Her first serious relationship had ended with her parents' death, because Paul hadn't wanted to be saddled with the guardianship of the twins.

"I don't love, Sarah."

"I'm not asking you to."

"Not now. But you will."

The surety in his tone bothered her in ways she didn't want to examine. She knew herself well enough to know she loved a challenge. But asking a man to love her, she knew better than to do that. "You are a little too sure of yourself for me."

He shrugged. "It's not that I think I'm so irresistible."

"Then what is it?" she asked.

"It's you," he said. Walking around her office he fiddled with the pictures on the wall showing various poses of her and the twins, her parents and the various members of the Taste of Home staff. Would he guess from the pictures that she treated her employees like family?

He walked out the door and she watched him go. Not sure if she'd had a near miss with something fatal or something too wonderful to live without.

Harris had never had luck with women. His mother had abandoned him when he was three. His father's two subsequent wives had quickly left as well. The longest relationship he'd had with a woman had lasted three weeks and by the end of that time he'd realized the truth for him about women. He was meant to live alone as a confirmed bachelor—non-family man. But deep inside he was tired of the silence.

Discovering that Sarah's brother had left and Ray had promised to give her a ride home shouldn't have come as a surprise to Harris. It seemed that if he kissed a woman and then made up his mind to do the noble thing, fate would of course intervene. All he wanted to do was to get as far away from Sarah as possible and to recover some of the control that he'd always taken for granted. Instead he found himself ensconced in the back of a dark limo with her.

Sarah stared out the window. It was the first time since they'd met that she had nothing to say. He searched his mind but small talk wasn't his forte.

"I've finally discovered a way to make you quiet."

"Happy?" she asked.

Since he was accustomed to silence, he should have been, but he wasn't. There was something sacrilegious about a hushed Sarah. He thought he might have hurt her and he regretted that because he'd never intended to make her feel bad about herself or anything that went on between them. But saying that out loud wasn't something he was comfortable with. "No."

She looked at him then and he wished she hadn't. Her eyes were wide and bruised. He knew the blame for that look lay squarely on his shoulders.

She'd taken the same seat in the limousine as she had the first time they'd met. Her skirt had pulled tight over her hips when she'd entered the car and he'd watched her with hungry eyes. Despite the intimacy they'd shared she was still a mystery to him.

"I don't know what you want from me, Harris," she said. He liked the way his name sounded when she said it. Wished that her voice didn't sound so husky though. This is why he should never have let Ray convince him to visit Taste of Home. He knew better. He'd spent thirty-five years learning that when it came to women he didn't have an M.B.A.

Damn. He didn't want to be having this conversation, though he felt compelled to be honest with her. Not that he'd planned to lie to her previously. "I don't know what I want from you either."

"That doesn't sound like you."

"How do you know?" he asked. They'd just met. They were still essentially strangers. No, that wasn't right. He knew her better than some of the woman he'd slept with. He knew she talked a lot except when she was nervous. He knew she nibbled her lower lip when she was unsure. He knew the sounds she made when he kissed her.

No, they weren't strangers.

"Your character is stamped on every move you make," she said at last.

He arched one eyebrow at her. How did a man respond to something like that? He hoped she really didn't know him as well as she'd just intimated because if she did, he was already in trouble. But then trouble and Sarah seemed to go hand in hand.

She moved next to him on the seat. She smelled faintly of Spring—flowers and rain and all the things

of rebirth. Never had he felt more like Hades—alone
and cold in his damp, dark underworld.

"I'm willing to meet you halfway," she said, placing her hand on his knee.

Her eyes sparkled with hope, he thought. Damn, he
knew then that he should break it off. Take her hand
off his leg and place it back on the seat between them.

But instincts older than common sense were in
charge now. He as still partially aroused from holding
her earlier and he hardened. If he moved her hand
anywhere it would be a few inches higher, he'd be in
heaven. "Halfway to what?"

"This thing between us."

Sarah wasn't like other women he knew, but suddenly she didn't seem so different. This was a relationship conversation. And he didn't know what he
was looking for from her but it wasn't a relationship.
He'd learned the hard way that Davidson men didn't
do the long-term man-woman thing very well. "I'm
leaving Thanksgiving weekend. I can't stay longer
even if I wanted to."

"We're talking vacation fling, right?" she asked.
She drew triangles on his thigh with her fingernail.
Her nails were painted a deep red color. The same
shade as American Beauty Roses. He knew roses because his father's obsession had been his rose garden.

Roses had the softest leaves. The only thing softer
had been Sarah's skin when he touched her. He
wanted to touch her again. To stop this conversation
in a physical way. His mouth on hers. The two of
them locked together, close as only a man and a

woman could be while the lights of the city flashed by beyond the windows.

"I'm not on vacation," he said, vaguely.

"Don't be obtuse." She moved her hand from his leg.

Control, Harris. He reminded himself. The problem here was simple. Sarah needed to know where he stood. And then she could decide if she wanted to spend time with him. A few weeks could be a hell of a memory, he thought. "It's hard not to be. Why are we having this conversation?"

She said nothing.

"Are you trying to justify coming to my hotel with me tonight? Because I can think of a better way to convince you than words."

Again silence.

"We're two adults contemplating an affair," he said.

"I'm not trying to justify it."

"Then what?" he asked, realizing he was willing to play her game to have one night with her.

Sarah had spent a long time alone. She dated when she had the time but it took a lot for a guy to make her want to leave the safety of her routine. Harris made her want to do that and it scared her because she knew a few weeks would be all they would share.

She was honest enough with herself to admit she sometimes used her family responsibilities as a barrier between her and the men who asked her out. At other times she used her obligations as a test. So far no man had ever measured up to her expectations. Honestly, she'd been okay with her situation until Harris had shattered the illusions of what she thought she'd wanted and made her realize that she'd forgotten her dream.

This conversation, his pointed questions, told a story. Was she trying to come up with a reason to go back to his hotel with him?

Sometimes she wondered if she wasn't looking for a man who didn't exist. That mythical Mr. Right, who'd be a lover, a partner and a friend. It seemed easy in books and movies and funny on television but the cold reality was—she was too much an optimist to say it—she knew the truth. There might not be a Mr. Right.

"I…I'm not too sure I know what I want from you, Harris." That much was true. She'd never felt so chaotic. This was crazy, he was a man. That was all. And despite her recent Magic 8-ball affirmation, she knew that it took more than cosmic luck for a man and woman to fall in love.

"Why make it difficult?" he asked.

He leaned toward her. Damn, he smelled so good. Clean, spicy—masculine. She shifted a little on the seat, trying to get closer to him without seeming to.

"Honestly, that's not what I'm doing. I expect more than an affair from the men I've involved in my life." Sarah had learned the hard way that unless you asked for what you wanted in life, you were often disappointed. Too bad she'd always been afraid to ask for what she really wanted.

He brushed his forefinger down the side her face stopping at the base of her neck. She wanted his mouth in just the same spot. Her skin tightened and her pulse quickened.

"An affair is all I have to give."

She shifted in her seat, pressing her legs together. She wished he'd stop touching her. No, that wasn't true. She wished he'd never stop touching her. But she didn't believe in lust at first sight. Ha, her inner conscience jeered. "I think it's clear we're on opposite sides here."

He dropped his hand. "Of course we are. That's probably why the yearning for you is sharp."

"You yearn for me?" she asked, surprised. It was the first time she felt like she'd glimpsed the real man under the facade of sophisticated charm.

"In ways you'll never know," he said, his gaze meeting hers. His eyes and hair reminded her of the Norse gods in the Viking legends she loved. But those men were tough, had had to be tough to survive and she longed to know what had shaped Harris. What events in his life had tempered the steel inside him and shaped him into who he was today?

She clenched her hands together to keep from touching him again. There were hidden depths to Harris Davidson. She knew it.

He had the potential to be more than a vacation affair. It was there in his eyes when he watched her. In his words when he said impossible things about yearning and made her believe that he could be her

Mr. Right. In his actions when he'd lit a fire inside her and put her needs in front of his.

"Oh, heck. I wish you hadn't said that."

"Honey, I figure my chances of seeing you after tonight are slim. There's no use in hedging."

"Why can't you commit to longer than your trip? Is it the distance?" she asked.

"I could lie to you and say it is."

"Then what?"

He glanced out the window, then ran his fingers through his thick hair. She remembered the texture of it under her hands. Her palms tingled and she wanted to touch him again.

"Tell me about your family."

"Why?"

"Just go with me here, okay?"

She didn't like talking about her parents because she still missed them. She still remembered the night they'd died and the night her life had changed so drastically. "My parents owned the restaurant until their death twelve years ago. That's when I took over raising the twins and the running the business."

"How'd your folks die?"

"Drunk driver. The twins and I were in the back seat of the car."

He patted her shoulder. She knew he meant the gesture as comfort and appreciated it. She still missed her parents. Especially now when the restaurant was facing an uncertain future and it was all that remained of her link to the past.

The house her parents had owned was too big and

too expensive for her to maintain so she'd had to sell it and move the twins to the small bungalow she could afford.

"I shouldn't have pried," he said.

"Why did you?"

"To make my point. Your parents loved each other, didn't they?"

"Of course. They wouldn't have married if they hadn't."

"You saw the good side of love. There is another side. A darker side and that's what my folks had."

"What's the darker side of love?" she asked. She thought maybe it was hate but that didn't seem right. No one married out of hate.

"Obsession."

"Who was obsessed?"

"My dad."

She didn't have words to say anything else. But she understood the point he'd made. His view of relationships made him leery. "I'm not asking you to sign an affidavit that says you'll marry me. I only want to know that you aren't using me."

He cupped her jaw in his hands as the limo coasted to a stop in front of her house. "I don't think I could use you."

She leaned up and kissed him gently backing away before passion could take control. "Want to come in for coffee?"

He pulled her closer and kissed her again. She had no control over the embrace and was swept away by the intensity of it. Ray opened the door and a cool breeze snaked through the car.

Harris let go of her and slid out of the car. He offered his hand to her and when she stood next to him outside the car, she felt like she was losing something precious.

"I'll call you."

He climbed back into the car without waiting for a response and she had the feeling she'd never hear from him again. Sarah made an important decision as the limousine drove away. Harris Davidson was a man who came along only once in a lifetime and she was willing to fight for him.

Four

Harris leaned back in the seat as they pulled away from Sarah's house. This business deal with the consortium was a straightforward takeover bid. And he struggled to keep it that way. He should be able to keep his attention there and if he was smart, he would get out of Orlando without seeing Sarah again.

Harris's first instinct was to return to the hotel room and keep to himself. Whenever that impulse struck he fought it. He didn't want to end up like his dad, spending fifteen years in an apartment somewhere and never leaving it.

He moved to the front of the limousine and lowered the partition. "You know any place to stop and get a drink?"

"Sure," Ray said.

"Women troubles?" Ray asked after a few minutes had passed.

"Nothing I can't handle," Harris said. And he believed it. He had a solid plan. Avoid Sarah until he left town. He could do that easily.

"Sarah looks a little feisty," Ray said.

"Ray, have you ever heard of employer-employee etiquette?"

"Nah, why am I breaching it?"

Harris raised one eyebrow at him. "Yes. And I don't appreciate it."

"Sorry, Mr. Davidson. I'm not a real formal guy."

"I've noticed."

"So, what about Sarah?" Ray asked.

Harris realized Ray wasn't going to stay in his role of driver. Harris started to put the partition up then stopped. Maybe this one time he could use an outside opinion. God, knew he didn't think around Sarah. Just turned into one big hormone.

"She has a way of shaking a man's concentration."

"The best ones do," Ray said.

"You married?" Harris asked.

"Nah...my line of work wasn't conducive to it."

Harris watched the driver. There was something in his voice that hinted at a feeling Harris understood too well. Something he refused to acknowledge in himself except deep in the night when no one was around to witness it. Something he'd tried to run from. Something he knew was loneliness.

"I've never had the inclination. There's something damned foolish about promising someone you'll spend your life together. Not even business deals last that long."

"I used to think like you do."

"What changed your mind?"

"A broad."

Harris chuckled. "Woman troubles?"

"*Madon',* you don't know the half of it. You going to call Sarah."

"I'm going to do what I should have done in the beginning."

"What's that?"

"Concentrate on business and forget about her."

"She didn't strike me as one of them shrews. Did she try to lecture you?"

"No."

"Ditzy?"

He thought about the Magic 8 ball she'd been playing with. Aside from that she seemed intelligent. Hell, he knew she was smart. Had seen it in her quick wit.

"If anything she's too smart."

Ray sighed and then pulled the limo to a stop on the shoulder. He pinched the bridge of his nose and then putting his arm along the back of the seat turned to him. "God knows I'm not an expert on relationships, but I'll tell you one thing, man. There's nothing like getting old and realizing you let the right one slip away."

Ray's words made a certain kind of sense, but all Harris could see was the Davidson family legacy in relationships. *Obsession.* It was a fatal weakness in the Davidson men. Harris had channeled that part of himself into making money. And he was damned good at it. He couldn't afford to have a woman like Sarah in his life.

The cell phone rang and Ray answered it.

He grunted a few times. Then said, "*Merda,* I'm trying."

Sounded like a fight was brewing. Harris moved to the rear of the car to give Ray some privacy. The driver made a lot of sense. He'd been protecting himself from relationships since he'd turned six. That was the year his father had a bout of depression. Harris had had to take care of the old man.

Sarah called to him. Called to the man he'd always wanted to be. Maybe he should give her one more chance. He was aching for her sweet warmth, though he knew he shouldn't reach out and take her. Yet he reached for his cell phone and called information. Three minutes later he had her number.

The phone rang four times before she picked up. "Hello."

Her voice was low and husky. Breathless as if she'd run to answer the call. He shouldn't have disturbed her. Nothing could come of this and he'd almost decided that he wasn't going to pursue her. A cold shower and solitary release would appease his body and if his soul hungered for something more from her…too bad.

"Is anyone there?"

He cleared his throat. "It's Harris."

"Oh, I didn't expect to hear from you again." He

heard her moving around in the background. The soft sounds of her footfalls on hardwood floors.

Ask her to dinner one more time, let her decline and then hang up. "I hadn't planned on calling."

"Why did you?"

"Dinner. I wanted to ask you to dinner." Yeah he was smooth and suave. Every woman's freaking dream come true.

"Dinner?" she asked. The rustle of cloth against cloth was muted in the background. What was she doing? His mind supplied an image of her changing.

He groaned silently, trying to ignore his imagination and concentrate on her words. She was going to be the death of him.

"It would have to be after the restaurant closes."

"I'll order something from room service."

"Why are you doing this, Harris?"

"I'm just asking you to dinner, Sarah. Millions of people share the meal every day."

"I'm just like a million others?"

No, she wasn't. And that was precisely why it was so important to him to that she say yes. He didn't say anything. Wouldn't give her the words he sensed she needed to say yes.

"I'm not sure about you."

"Have dinner with me?"

"Dinner won't change anything," she said quietly.

"I never thought it would."

"What did you think then?"

"That you'd be my downfall."

"Harris."

"I'll send Ray for you when the restaurant closes."

"Okay."

He hung up before she could say anything else. He knew he had one shot at making this evening one to remember. There could never be more than one night for them because she awakened in him all those feelings that his father had described to him. All those feelings that made his career pale in comparison. All those feelings that he'd vowed to never experience.

Sarah was not having a good day. She'd been to the high school twice today. First for Burt who had been called to the office for fighting. Then for Isabella, her sister, who had ripped her skirt and needed a new one. The main oven in the kitchen wouldn't get hotter than 250 degrees and she'd just received a rather ominous letter from her landlord informing her that the strip mall had been sold and that she'd be contacted by the new owners shortly about a new lease agreement.

All in all she thought it didn't bode well for her date with Harris later that evening. She'd wanted to have a pedicure and maybe buy something new to wear but there didn't seem to be time or money. The lights of the city flashed past the windows of the limo as Ray drove her to the Dolphin hotel on Disney property. She'd been there one time to a karaoke bar with some friends.

There was a single red rose on the seat left for her and a note in his own handwriting that said. *The evening awaits.*

Her first impulse had been to order Ray to turn the car around and take her home. She had no idea what he expected from her. Well, okay she had a small inkling but she'd realized last night sleeping in the same bed she'd slept in since she was a child that she wasn't ready for Harris. Harris represented change to her and she'd just gotten comfortable with herself.

She hated riding in the back of the car by herself. It left too much time to think and her thoughts weren't as pleasant as usual. She lowered the partition between the front and back.

"Yes, ma'am?" Ray asked. His voice was gravelly and low and she wondered what he'd done before he'd driven a limo because there was something in his face that hinted at more.

"How's it going tonight, Ray?"

He bit on the cigar stump in his mouth, talking around it. "Not bad."

"How'd you get into the limo service?" she asked.

"Just kind of fell into it."

"What did you do before?" she asked.

"This and that."

"Don't want to talk about it?" she asked. Ray had the look of a man who'd lived a rough and lonely life. She worried that years from now Harris might have that some look about him.

"How'd you guess?"

"I'm not as ditzy as I might appear at times."

He chuckled. The sound made Sarah smile. One of her gifts was making people feel good.

"What do you know about Harris? Have you driven him for long?"

"This is the first time."

"Oh. So you wouldn't know if this is his M.O."

He coasted to a stop in I-4 traffic and met her gaze in the mirror. "What's that mean?"

"Nothing. I'm just doubting myself," she said, more to herself than to Ray.

"Why?" he asked.

She didn't want to vocalize her insecurity. "Why not? I mean I'm not sophisticated or successful and Harris reeks of those things."

"Maybe that's part of your appeal."

"You think so?"

"I'm sure it is. Don't sell yourself short, Sarah. You're a very attractive woman." Ray turned his attention to the road and a short while later they arrived at the hotel. Ray winked at her as he opened the door and Sarah felt…still unsure.

She wasn't the kind of woman who met men for dinner in their hotel rooms. No matter how attractive they might be. She hesitated in the lobby. Maybe she'd have Ray take her home. She'd call Harris from the car.

She pivoted.

"Sarah?"

"Hello, Harris."

"Damn, I wanted to be here when you arrived but the elevator was slow."

He appeared nervous. Not at all the calm self-assured man she'd come to know. That made her feel better in a hundred ways.

"Ready for dinner?" he asked.

She stared at him not really sure. He looked different tonight. No five-hundred-dollar-suit to make him stand apart from the others milling around the lobby. Yet he did stand apart. Something in his icy-gray eyes told her that getting close to this man would be nearly impossible.

His deceptively casual clothes and intense gaze. The keen intelligence and the weariness that she was coming to understand were part of who he was. His shirt was a cream silk one open at the neck and tucked into a pair of jeans that were so old and faded they clung to his skin like a lover. She drew in a deep a breath as awareness rolled over her.

There was no kidding herself that she had an altruistic goal here. No pretending that teaching Harris to love was her only motivator. She wanted him.

And she knew her heart. Knew it well. There was a reason why she kept going to church each week and lighting candles in the hopes of finding a man. She wanted to believe the things that life had shown her didn't exist. She wanted to find the happiness in life. The type of happiness she experienced every time a couple fell in love in a movie. She wanted to believe in the illusion that Harris so effortlessly wove around her.

He took her arm and led her to the bank of elevators. His touch swept through her body like fire over dry land. She trembled under the impact and acknowledged that maybe she was here for a very physical reason. It had been a long time since she'd had a lover.

His hand slid down her arm and he slid his fingers between hers. He squeezed gently and she glanced up at him and smiled. There was something so different about Harris tonight.

"Ready?"

"Yes," she said, realizing she was starting an adventure.

Harris's room overlooked Epcot center. He'd never been to the theme park despite numerous visits to central Florida. He didn't believe in deception and fantasy and saw no point in wasting his money. He liked the Dolphin hotel because it was set up along the lines of many of the Japanese places he stayed while traveling in Asia.

But seeing Sarah against the backdrop of make believe made him realize how different they both were. His father had chased an illusion and ended up locked alone in his apartment. It was a warning Harris couldn't ignore.

His suite was comprised of a sitting area with a sofa and love seat. A desk where he worked and then a bedroom with a large king-size bed.

"This doesn't look like a hotel room," she said.

"I travel so often that I take the luxuries I'm used to with me."

"You bring furniture?"

"Just bookcases."

"You like to read?"

Like was too soft a word to describe his love of books. But he refused to sound like a geek in front of her. Why what she thought of him was so important, he didn't know, he only knew that it was. "Yes."

"Me, too."

She skimmed her finger along the edges of the hardcover books. New releases sat next to hundred-year-old classics. His tastes were eclectic when it came to reading.

"I love this one," she said, pausing next to a new title by Nick Hornby, the British author.

"I haven't read it yet." Sometimes Harris felt himself living vicariously through novels. For the most part he read family dramas and relationship books. And he was too honest with himself not to admit that those stories were as close as he wanted to come to experiencing those bonds.

"If you like his other titles you'll enjoy this one," she said. She watched him closely and his neatly laid plans started to shatter. There was something in her eyes that told him she wasn't buying his casual pose. She wasn't going to settle for the surface Harris that the women he'd had affairs with in the past had.

Harris didn't want to talk about books or likes. He wanted to keep Sarah in a neat little compartment. Not allow himself to know her too well. Just tease himself a little with the intense sexuality she brought to the surface. Tease himself with her warm smile and imagine for these few brief weeks that he was a man worthy of that smile.

"Let's sit down and eat. I hope you like Japanese food. I ordered box dinners for us. Nothing too sophisticated."

"Love them. You should try Ichiban downtown," she said with a smile.

He led her to the table set up in front of the bank of windows. Fiddling with the Bose CD player on the coffee table Harris filled the room with Mozart. There was something soothing about the classical composer. He joined Sarah at the table.

He poured them both a glass of sake and then lifted his glass toward her.

"To serendipity," she said.

He clinked his glass to hers. He didn't believe in things like that but he took a sip anyway.

"Why serendipity?" he asked as she toyed with her chopsticks.

She set them down and bit her lower lip. She's nervous, he thought.

"It brought us together," she said at last.

"How can you be sure?" he asked, brushing his finger down the side of her face. He thought maybe some sort of karma from a past life was dogging him. Putting him in the path of this woman who tempted him to forget the truths he knew about himself and about life.

"What else would you call it?" she asked, tilting her head to the side. The cool strands of her thick hair brushed the back of his hand. He wanted to twist his wrist and wrap his hand in the silky stuff. Use that grip to bring her head closer to his and plunder her mouth. To make her forget about why they met and to stop talking about things that couldn't be proven.

"Bad luck," he said at last.

"Bad?" She shifted to the side breaking the contact with his hand.

"Your car was broken down," he reminded her, rubbing his fingers together and picking up his chopsticks. They felt hard and coarse after the smoothness of her skin.

"But something good came of it."

"Our meeting," he said, sensing she was going to say it.

She nodded. He wasn't sure what else to say to her. Didn't she understand that chance meetings weren't ordained by fate but by routine.

"I'm not sure it's a good thing," he said at last.

"Why not?"

"Let's eat dinner first. We can talk later."

She looked like she was going to argue but she acquiesced.

"This is your routine?" she asked after they'd finished the main course.

"Pretty much that is my life," he said, gesturing to his computer.

"I knew you were a workaholic."

"So are you," he reminded her.

She glanced around the room. "Where are the pictures of your family?"

"I don't have a family."

"No family? Test-tube baby?"

"Nothing so sci-fi. I had a mother and my father is still alive."

"Then you have a family."

Family was that image you conjured in your head of a mom and dad and couple of kids. Harris had never had anything close to that. "Not that counts."

"Do you want to talk about it?" she asked tilting her head to the side. He knew she wanted to offer him comfort but he didn't want her pity. He wanted her passion.

"Would that make you more comfortable?"

"I don't know. You know a lot about me. I don't even know what you do for a living."

He made money for people with lots of money but that never sounded nice. "I'm a financial consultant."

"With a Harvard M.B.A."

"See you know more than you think you do." This was better. He slid his foot between hers under the table and she arched her eyebrows at him but didn't move away.

"Why don't you consider your father family?"

Harris pulled his foot back. Seduction was one thing but baring his soul to Sarah wasn't something he was prepared to do. His father—damn he should never have brought the man up. "He's...different."

"How?" she asked.

He wasn't saying any more on the topic. He didn't want her to really understand how messed up he was when it came to relationships. But Sarah reached out and clasped his clenched fist in one of her small hands. She rubbed her finger across the back of his knuckles and he had a glimpse of what might be. That glimpse was enough for him to unclench his hand and look into Sarah's eyes.

Why should this one woman make him react so strongly when no other one ever had?

"He can't cope with life. He never leaves his apartment." Harris felt foolish saying the words out loud but because he wanted Sarah in his bed he owed her a little truth. Seduction was never about truth. Only about wants and needs.

"Oh, Harris."

"I told you my past is all about the darker side of love."

"What about the present?"

"What about it?"

"Am I only an obsession?" she asked.

"I can't decide," he said, standing and pulling her in his arms. He lowered his head to hers and took the kiss that he'd been waiting a lifetime to taste.

Five

Sarah knew she should get out of that hotel suite as fast as her legs could carry her but she wasn't going anywhere. Harris's arms around her felt right in a way that nothing had since her parents' death twelve long years ago. Too right. And she knew her vulnerabilities better than most women did. She faced them every night when she closed down the restaurant that she fought to save even though working there was a life sentence.

She knew that she was waiting for a man like Harris. That she'd been praying for a guy like him since before she was old enough to realize that real-life seldom resembled fiction. And her one true weakness was that she longed for someone to watch over her. Someone big and strong who'd be willing to help shoulder her burdens—not all the time just once in a while.

She slid away from Harris even though all she wanted to do was rip off her dress and say take me, big boy. Emotionally she stepped back as well. Reaching up she smoothed her hair and tried to make some appearance of normalcy even though her pulse was racing to beat the band.

She and Harris had some unfinished business before things went too much further. Because when he'd held her just a moment earlier she'd realized she already cared about this man with the dark stormy eyes. She already cared about this man who made her forget that happy endings didn't seem in the cards for her. She already cared for this man who was watching her as if she'd turned into a deadly enemy.

Nerves assailed her and for once she couldn't talk. He kept watching her, making her more nervous with each passing second. She shrugged and tried to say something but all that emerged was a squeak.

Harris cursed under his breath. "I need a drink."

He paced to the liquor cabinet and poured himself a whiskey. She watched him unsure what to do next. Watching Harris drink wasn't it.

She walked around him to the love seat facing the windows. Patting the cushion next to her, she said, "Come join me."

"I think I'd rather take this news standing up," he said, tossing back his drink.

"I'm not going to be delivering a proclamation."

"Then what?"

"I want to finish our conversation from earlier."

"Is that really necessary?"

She thought about it. To Harris life was an endless cycle of affairs. The whole evening had the feeling of ritual. Seductive though it was to think that Harris had pulled out all the romantic stops for her tonight, his posture said otherwise. He'd done this before and she needed to feel like she wasn't one of the many with Harris. Because he wasn't one of many to her. "To me it is."

He sighed and ran his fingers through his blond hair. She wished she'd had the guts to run her fingers through it. She wished she'd held his head in her hands and plundered his mouth instead of being a slave to his embrace. She wished, just once, she'd have the courage to be the woman she'd always dreamed of.

Maybe tonight.

"You said something about our meeting being bad luck."

He poured himself another splash of whiskey and knocked it back like medicine. Cursing again he paced to the wall of windows just as the fireworks started lighting up the sky. How would seeing relationships as obsessions affect a man?

It was odd to see Harris illuminated by the fireworks. He was too grounded. To nose-to-the-grindstone. Maybe that's why their paths crossed, she thought. Maybe she was meant to show him the lighter side of life.

"I'm not sure you want to hear my thoughts on luck," he said after a few minutes.

"But I do."

He pivoted to face her and she couldn't make out his features in the shadows of the candlelight room. But she knew he was sincere. When had he ever not been?

"Relationships—and I'm speaking strictly of business ones here—are hard to maintain. And then you have a common goal."

"Men and women don't?"

"Not in my experience."

"You keep saying that. But Harris, you aren't your father."

"I know that," he said.

She wanted to probe deeper but suddenly was afraid to. "I think we can be different."

"Why do you think that? Is it a sop for your conscience to justify sleeping with me?" he asked. Sarcasm was his defense mechanism, she noticed.

She was willing to cut him some slack but she didn't want to be a doormat. "That was low, even for you."

He paced back to the liquor cabinet but didn't pour anything, just toyed with his empty glass.

"I'm sorry," he said, at last.

"Do you really feel that way?" she asked.

"God, no. I don't want to talk about this any more tonight. I'm not sure any kind of luck exists. But if it does…"

She left the couch and went to his side. "If it does?"

"Then I'm hoping we've got some kind of good karma working for us. The last thing I want to do is hurt you."

"Oh, Harris."

He didn't say anything else, just pulled her into his arms and kissed her with a desperation she sensed he'd deny.

His mouth moved over hers with surety and purpose and she knew that he was intent tonight on…what? Seduction seemed the most likely course. The evening was a prelude to it. A perfect dinner with soft candlelight and romantic music.

But she knew that there was more at work here than seduction. His words echoed in her mind…I don't want to hurt you. It scared her that he already knew he could hurt her. The only consolation she took was that there was genuine longing in his eyes that made her glow with all her femininity. Made her feel like the only woman on earth who could tame the wildness in his soul.

Reaching up, she cupped his face. She ran her fingers along his jaw and then to the back of his neck and over his shoulders. They were strong and capable. Everything about him was. And she flexed her fingers, testing the resiliency of those muscles.

His mouth left her, tracking a wet path down her neck, stopping to suck the pulse point at the base of her neck. His touch shot sensations straight to her groin and she shifted against him. Needing him in ways and in places she hadn't just a moment before.

"Harris," she said, softly clasping his face in both her hands.

He glanced up at her. She saw in his eyes too many emotions to identify and she felt in the pit of her stomach a feeling of nervous excitement.

"No more talking tonight," he said, covering her lips with one finger.

He rubbed his forefinger over her lips. Teasing her until she opened them and tasted him with the tip of her tongue. She bit lightly on his finger. His eyes darkened. Emotion was shunted aside by a more primal response. He grabbed her hips and tugged her body closer to his until not even an inch of space remained between them.

She took his jaw in her hands and pulled his face down to hers. His pupils were dilated and between her legs she felt him hot and hard. She'd never experienced a tenth of this passion with other men.

His growled deep in his throat and lowered his head to hers again. This time there was no gentle seduction but a full out taking of her mouth. He didn't mask what he wanted—he took. And she let him.

One of his hands left her waist and cupped her butt, pulling her closer until her mound rested against his hardness. She ceased thinking.

His mouth slid down her neck, suckling at the base. Her breasts felt so full and achingly tight. She leaned into his chest, trying to alleviate the pressure, which only heightened with each pull of his mouth on her neck.

He moaned and she felt the sound throughout her body. His other hand left her back and found her aching nipple. Rubbing through the thin layers of dress and bra, he brought relief to the aching flesh.

Sarah threw her head back. His other hand slid under her skirt, up her leg. Not stopping until he reached the center of her. She moaned again as his fingers skimmed the edge of her panties and slid underneath.

Circling the slick flesh between her legs, he teased her with the promise of more. She shifted herself against his touch and finally felt him at the entrance of her body. He thrust two fingers deep inside her and she clutched at his shoulders.

His thumb rubbed at the center of her pleasure and fire stormed through her. Throwing her closer and closer to the pinnacle. Her breathing increased, she could scarcely catch her breath. His hand on her bottom held her hips steady as he rocked against her.

Her nerves all tightened. Everything inside her clenched and then there was the release she'd been driving toward. She shivered in the aftermath. Harris was still rock-hard between her legs. But he wrapped his arms around her and lowered his leg from between her own.

His hands rubbed slowly up and down her back. She looked up at him. His face was flushed, his breathing still too rapid.

She reached between their bodies, wanting to share

the same release he'd given her with him. But he stopped her.

"Why?"

"Because we need the bed for what I have in mind," he said, scooping her up and carrying her down the short hall into the darkened bedroom. He set her on her feet.

"Don't move."

"Yes, sir," she said.

"I like the sound of respect in the bedroom," he said. He switched on the light on the nightstand. The room was still mostly shadows with a great cone of light in the center. Sarah hovered on the edge of the darkness. Feeling too exposed in this room. It seemed all her dreams and desires were bared to him.

"Into domination?" she asked, lightly. Trying to mask her own deepest needs. She didn't want him to know that she needed him with a desperation she'd never felt before. She wasn't sure of herself at all with Harris.

"No. But lately I've been obsessed with getting into you." His words were a rasp in the shadowy room. They brushed over her aroused senses like a mink glove and she shivered, needing to be in his arms again.

"Really?" she asked, giving up the pretense that she wanted to be anywhere but here with him. She couldn't believe that this worldly man needed anything from her—Sarah Malcolm and not just any woman. She remembered what Ray had said earlier that maybe part of her appeal to Harris was that she wasn't like the women he was used to. Suddenly she very glad for that.

He took her hand and carried it to his crotch. All thoughts other than ones about primal mating left her mind. He pulsed against her. She slid her fingers along his zipper caressing him. He moaned deep in his throat.

"Don't doubt that this is real," he said.

She measured him with her hand. His hips rocked against her and she tightened her grip. She couldn't wait to touch his naked flesh. "I'm not."

"This might be all I have to give you," he said.

"I'm betting that I can make you believe in something more."

"I can't make any promises," he said.

The fireworks continued to echo in the night and she stared up at his dear face in the dark room. "I'm only asking for one tonight."

He watched her. "What's that?"

"Make me yours," she said, standing on tiptoe and wrapping her arms around his neck.

Harris had glimpsed the dark underbelly of his soul only twice in his life. The first time he'd been six and clinging desperately to his mother's legs as she'd walked out of the Connecticut mansion they'd called home. The second time he'd been a young man of twenty-one and he'd pleaded with Mona to give them one more chance. Tonight as he held Sarah in his arms he realized that he was tempted to make her say she'd never leave him.

Damn it. She didn't mean anything to him. He wouldn't let her. This was an affair nothing more. *Nothing less.* He should have offered to make her his mistress. He'd have felt better about their affair knowing all his cards were on the table.

They'd talked too much already tonight. In the morning he'd make sure she understood everything. Her soft breath brushed against his neck. He didn't want to believe what he saw in Sarah's eyes—the knowledge that she thought this was more than an affair.

He was the master of illusion and tonight he was the embodiment of his training. Suave, sophisticated—an experienced man who wanted only to share a night filled with pleasure with the woman in his arms.

He'd meant for this to be sweet seduction but he had needed her too badly. Needed to brand her as his if only for this short time. She felt fragile and very feminine in his hands. Though he refused to acknowledge that he might have the power to hurt her. Instead he swept his hands over her body, removing her clothing as he went.

"No," she said, her small hands captured his wrists.

Startled, he stopped. He was surprised she was stopping now but he'd always bent to a lady's wishes. If Sarah wanted to call a halt now—he'd acquiesce.

Leaning up on tiptoe, she brushed the softest kiss against his jaw. His life had been hard by nature and experience. Even his sexual encounters had owed more to physical desire than to any longing for physical touching. But her kiss was different.

"This time I want you with me," she said.

"I will be, baby." No doubt about it. He might even be before her if they didn't stop talking and get into bed.

"I'm not taking any chances."

She unbuttoned his shirt and pushed it to the floor. "That first day we met…in the limo…I had a fantasy of you without your shirt in bed."

"Really? I only had my shirt off?"

"Hmm-mmm. At least in the beginning. I don't want to rush things between us. Not this first time."

"I'm all about indulging fantasies," he said, knowing he wasn't. But tonight he wanted to be her white knight. Tonight he wanted to pretend his armor hadn't been tarnished. Tonight was all for Sarah. He walked over to the bed and sprawled on his back arms out to his sides.

"How's this?"

"Just about perfect," she said. She sat next to him on the bed, tracing her fingers over the muscles of his chest.

Her touch burned through the layers of skin and he felt it bone deep. Sensation spread throughout his body and his nipples tightened and his groin was so full and heavy he felt his pulse down there. He needed to be inside her now. No more playing. No more waiting.

He captured her in his arms and took her mouth. Tasted her deeply while he removed her clothing with more efficiency than skill. Only when her clothes were in a pile at their feet at the bottom of the bed and they were laying naked chest to breasts did he stop. He felt the humid warmth of her center through the fabric of his trousers. He had to stop and breathe deeply to keep from spilling himself in his pants.

He opened his eyes and looked up at her dark chocolate gaze. Watched the passion on her face as she undulated against him. She was so responsive, she went to his head like his first sip of liquor. She made him feel like the first man to ever awaken a woman to her sensuality and the experience was a heady one.

He slid his hands over her back, following the line of her spine. He cupped her butt and held her hips still while he thrust up against her. He wished he'd taken the time to open his fly so he could feel her wetness against his skin.

She moaned deep in her throat and he felt his grip on his control slip. Leaning up, he captured her nipple in his mouth and suckled her. He shifted them on the bed so they were both on their sides. Her fingers tunneled through his hair holding him closer to her. He massaged her other breast, plucking at the hardened nipple before switching to it and taking it in his mouth as well.

Her nails scraped lightly down his back and she worked her hands between them. Opening his pants and shoving them down his legs with his boxers, he kicked free of the fabric and the first touch of Sarah's hands on his penis was like fire. He shuddered under her touch. She cupped him with one hand and stroked the length of his erection with the other.

He lifted his head from her breast and sprawled on his back, widening his legs to give her more room to explore him.

"Was this part of your fantasy?" he asked, desperately trying to hold on and give her the time she'd asked for to explore him.

"Not until much later that night," she said.

She bent and nibbled at his chest, tracing the line of hair with her tongue until she reached the part of him she still cupped in her hands. He was so hard, so ready that her touch was torture yet he made no move to stop her as she sampled him with her mouth.

His hips jerked at her touch against his will. "I can't wait any longer."

"Then don't," she said.

"Are you on the pill?"

"I...yes, I am."

"I'm clean. Give blood regularly."

"So am I," she said. But she'd stopped touching him.

"Now that that's out of the way," he said, pushing her on her back and caressing her from shoulders to toes and back again. Only when she was twisting on the bed, did he slide up over her.

He tested her readiness with his hand at her center, finding the tender bud that was her pleasure center and fondling it lightly until she grabbed his shoulders and pulled him over her. "Now, Harris."

He smiled as he positioned himself and slid into

her. Her body resisted at first. He went as slowly as he could giving her time to adjust to his length. But his control was on a hair-trigger and when she leaned up and put her mouth against his chest, right over his damned heart, he began to thrust.

He knew it was too soon for her. Too much for her to be comfortable with. Using his hands he brought her along as best he could. Soon her hips were rising frantically against his. He waited for the sound he heard earlier in the living room. That catching of her breath and a long, low moan that signaled her release. As soon as he heard it, he slid his arms under thighs and pushed her legs back, opening her to deeper thrusts. He slammed into two more times before he felt that tingling in the back of his spine and he emptied his body into hers, calling her name.

She shivered and convulsed again underneath him. He rolled to his side, taking her with him. Tucking her face against his neck he kept their bodies connected because he realized he'd just had a glimpse of heaven on earth and he wasn't ready to let it go.

Six

Sarah had never slept in any bed other than her own since she'd become an adult. Harris's was luxurious. The sheets his own and not the hotel's. She rolled over and buried her face in the pillow, inhaling deeply. She reached for Harris and encountered an empty bed.

She rolled to her side and opened her eyes. It was a little before seven in the morning. It was a Saturday and often the only day she got to sleep in because she had church on Sunday.

She pulled the sheet more firmly around herself. Florida sun light filled the room, leaving her nowhere to hide. Not from herself or from Harris. But he was already gone and she had only her own self-doubts to face this morning.

She shivered a little at the direction of her thoughts.

She needed to take action and get herself together. Why was she worrying anyway? Harris was probably in the shower or getting breakfast for them.

Oh, God. What if he'd already left the suite and she was here alone? Last night he'd said no promises and glibly she'd agreed to that but this morning, with the sun shining brightly, she realized she needed promises. She needed something more from him.

It reminded her too much of Paul and when he'd left her. She felt inadequate and small. But she wasn't that girl anymore. She was a woman now. And she wasn't going to hide in this bed all day.

She searched the floor for her clothes and dressed quickly. Her skirt and shirt were rumpled and wrinkled and she felt unkempt. She was clearly not the type of woman who was cut out to lead the single lifestyle. Even her clothes weren't up to the task. She'd watched *Sex and the City*—those girls usually looked good the morning after.

"Morning," Harris said from the doorway. His husky voice brushed over her senses making her aware of him. He'd showered and shaved and he looked like a Viking raider this morning. His eyes as cold as the North Sea.

He held a few items in her hands but she didn't notice what they were. She noticed that he didn't look her in the eye and that he didn't glance at the bed. Regrets. She thought she'd be the only one with them this morning.

"Good morning," she said, reaching up to pat her hair down. The curse of naturally curly hair was that it always looked like a fright wig in the morning. She refused to glance at the mirror to confirm her image. It didn't seem fair that he looked ready for a photo shoot with *GQ* and she felt like a *fashion don't.*

"I brought you some things," he said. He had face soap, a toothbrush and some toothpaste in his hands.

"Thanks."

She reached for the toothbrush. But he didn't hand it to her. Instead, he reached up and tucked one of her curls behind her ear. And she felt the first ray of hope she'd experienced since waking up alone. His caress was light, so light she was afraid she'd imagined it.

She swallowed trying to think of the right thing to say. The right words that would convince Harris that maybe they had a chance at something more than just sex. The right words that would leave her dignity intact.

"Damn, you feel so good."

She started to close the space between them. To reach for him and take him back to bed with her. That was the one place where they seemed to be on the same page.

But he took a step back. She felt like he'd slapped her in the face. Wrapping her arms around her waist, she glanced around for her purse. And couldn't find it. She paced past, Harris into the living room. There it was.

"Dammit, Sarah. I promised myself I wouldn't take you again."

"Why?" she asked, wondering if he had some kind of one night rule.

"I think we need to talk." He rubbed his hand over his face. Maybe this wasn't a routine thing for him either?

"I don't like the sound of that," she said, carefully.

"I don't like the thought of that. I'd rather keep you in my bed all weekend."

Earlier she'd have agreed to it but her emotions, the ones she'd carefully kept hidden since Paul walked out on her, warned her that she was getting too involved with Harris. "I'm not objecting."

"Yes, you are. You'd be worried about your siblings and your restaurant."

"When you touch me I can't think."

"Don't say things like that. I'm trying to be noble."

There was seriousness to his words that touched her soul. "You don't have to try."

"Hell, yes I do."

She'd noticed how hard he drove himself. Last night he'd gotten out of bed in the middle of the night to work. She'd found him and brought him back but it had shown exactly where his mind lay. Exactly where he felt the most comfort and exactly where he felt the most secure. "You're too hard on yourself."

He grunted. What did that mean? Why did men respond like that when they didn't want to pursue a line of conversation?

Sarah made a quick decision. "I can't talk like this. I need a shower and clean clothes."

He nodded. "I'll call down to Ray and have him take you home. We can meet later for lunch. Is your car working again?"

"My car's fine."

"Lunch then?"

She started to agree. But she realized there was something very distant about Harris this morning. His conversation said he wanted to get to know her a little better but his body language said…was he afraid of getting hurt?

"Why don't you come home with me? I'll fix us a nice breakfast and we can talk there."

Harris wasn't sure exactly how he ended up at the small bungalow Sarah called home but here he was. On the back patio surrounded by her family and his driver. Ray was a strange little man—kind of funny but with weird silences. Harris was uncomfortable sharing a meal with staff but Sarah had given him a look that said he better get over it.

Ray didn't look too pleased, either. He'd gotten another call on his cell phone when they'd arrived and Harris had overheard him say *leave me alone, dammit, I'm doing the best I can.*

There was more to his driver than Harris wanted to know. He liked keeping people in their places. But Sarah was making him realize that people had lives outside of their jobs. He'd always known that but now she was letting him see it and he wasn't sure he liked this new vision.

Why pleasing Sarah was so important to him he didn't analyze. He only knew that it was.

When they arrived at her house he got a surprise. Harris hadn't realized that Burt was a twin or that Isabella would look just like Sarah.

This glimpse into her life and her close-knit family made him feel even more the outsider. Made him realize that the distance he'd been using to supposedly protect Sarah was really there to protect him. Seeing their happy family, Harris was more determined than ever not to end up like his dad, alone in an apartment afraid to care because he'd been hurt too many times.

"Catch you later, man," Burt said, disappearing through the house.

"Burt, I need a ride to the Y."

"Shake a leg, Bella. I'm not your taxi service."

Harris heard them bantering until the front door closed behind them.

"My life is craziness," Sarah said.

She'd showered and changed after they had arrived at her house. Now he regretted letting her leave his suite. He understood his father a little better at this moment. There was something to be said for that kind of aloneness. The kind that left a man feeling in control of his world. The kind that made him realize how superficial the life he'd been leading was.

Ray's cell phone rang again. He glanced at the number and pitched the phone into Sarah's pool. For the first time that day his driver smiled with unholy glee.

"What was that about?" Sarah asked.

"Certain people are too hands-on," Ray said, leaned back in his chair and calmly took a sip of his espresso.

"Your boss?"

"Yeah. I knew this new job was going to be a pain in the ass."

"That's why I started my own business," Harris said.

"You worked for someone else?" Sarah asked.

"For a few years," he said.

"Why?" she asked.

"I needed to learn the ropes."

"Did you?"

"Yeah, as much as it chafed taking orders in the office I did it."

"Smart man," Ray said.

"He's an M.B.A. from Harvard."

"That's okay. He's got street smarts, too."

"Do you?" Sarah asked.

"I've never lived on the streets," Harris said, not really wanting to talk about his life.

"Yeah but you're no babbeo."

"Babbeo?"

Ray scratched his head and shrugged. "I don't have an American word I can use in mixed company."

"Wimp?" Sarah suggested.

Ray winked at Sarah. "Not exactly what I was thinking, but yeah, wimp works."

"I learned early you can only count on yourself," Harris said. He liked working for himself. He knew his own limitations and had made his business successful by driving hard toward his goals. He didn't have to worry about other people's weaknesses only his own. And he was intimately acquainted with those.

"Amen," Ray said.

Ray's pager started going off and he glanced at the LCD screen and cursed under his breath. "I'll be in the car."

Sarah watched Ray leave and then turned back toward him. "Do you really think you can only count on yourself?"

"Yes." He'd had three administrative assistants in the fifteen years he'd been in business for himself. He'd learned that those people worked hard but the ultimate loyalties lay elsewhere—not with him or his company. Once he'd figured that out he'd been able to manage more effectively.

"Seems like a lonely way to live," she said.

"I'm content—what more can a man ask for?" Harris said.

"What about family?"

"I prefer things I can measure with a spreadsheet," he said. He'd learned a long time ago that the ability to count losses was an important one.

"I'll take family."

He didn't like the path this conversation was on. There was no way he was going to be able convince her his viewpoint was right. Her life had been different than his. Even the loss of her parents hadn't warped her the way his dad's behavior had shaped his life. "But you also have your business."

"That was really my parents' dream. I'm just keeping it going for them."

"Are they coming back?" he asked, curious what she meant.

"No. I just want everything to be right for Burt and Isabella," she said, her voice telling him she wasn't sure herself why she had kept the restaurant going.

He didn't know any other woman who could handle herself in so many different situations. But Sarah wasn't sure she could. The irony wasn't lost on him and he vowed to make sure she didn't doubt herself anymore. If he left her with nothing else, he'd leave her with confidence.

"What about your dreams?" he asked at last.

"My dreams?"

"Yeah, your dreams. Don't you have any?" Harris reached across the table and caressed her face.

"Of course I do. Everyone does."

"What are they?"

"Are you sure you want to hear this?"

"Now who's afraid to let the other person in?"

"Touché."

She bowed her head and reached for her coffee cup. Then set it aside. He wondered what her dreams were that she was afraid to share them with him.

Trust me, he wanted to say. But he knew better. "Tell me."

"You'll laugh."

"Never."

"Promise?"

He just stared at her.

She sighed. "I just wanted to be a wife and mother. My dreams were to find Mr. Right and raise kids with him. I know it's not PC to say that but that's all I want but…"

"Why haven't you pursued your dream?" he asked. Knowing he'd never fill her ideal for the perfect mate. He wasn't sure why he even cared. He was leaving for the West Coast in a few weeks. Why did it matter that even if he stayed he still wouldn't be her Mr. Right?

"I have to keep the restaurant going and no guy wants to help raise someone else's kids."

"Your brother and sister are almost out of the nest," he said. She wasn't telling him everything, he could tell there wasn't something more behind her words.

"You said it was your dream," he said.

"Well…it's just that I've raised a family—Burt and Isabella—and I'm not sure that's what I want to do again."

"So what do you want to do?"

"I'm not sure."

He knew Sarah better than that. "Trust me, Sarah. Tell me your dream."

She swallowed and fiddled with the fork in front of her. "I haven't told anyone."

That made him feel good in a way he knew it shouldn't have. "Tell me."

"I want to open my own bakery."

"Why can't you do it now?"

"I told you, I have to keep my parents' dream alive for my siblings."

"What about—"

"Enough about me. Don't you ever wish for a family of your own?"

"No. Too many variables. I like things I can measure."

"People can't be measured," she said.

He raised one eyebrow at her. She'd just measured him and all mankind and found them lacking. But he didn't say that to her.

"I just meant that you sometimes are surprised by a person."

"Usually when they've let you down."

"Emotionally."

"I thought you said I wasn't a wimp."

"Emotion doesn't equal wimp."

He knew otherwise. "I meant in business."

"Isn't there more to life than business?" she asked.

"No." He'd learned the hard way that business was the only thing he could count on.

"I think you're afraid."

Harris flexed his muscles. He didn't like the thought of having weaknesses or Sarah noticing them. "Of what?"

"Finding out you're wrong."

"I can admit when I'm wrong."

"But if you were wrong about people it would mean your entire life was built around an illusion."

"Who's to say your life isn't?"

"I'm happy," she said.

"Good for you. I'm successful and respected. I lead a life most men would envy."

"Is it enough?" she asked. She had her hands clenched on the table in front of her and he wanted to say no. But he wasn't going to be that weak. Not now. Not with her. He needed to get back to work. Back to the environment where he was in control. Back to the one place where he knew all the variables and could react accordingly.

"Most days," he said, standing and walking out of her garden. Out of the little Eden she'd created with her home and her words and her soft eyes that beckoned him to taste the apple she held in her hand. Only this time the apple would bring man into Eden not expel him from it. And he knew he wasn't meant to live in Eden.

"I thought we were going to talk about us," she said, following him.

"Is there an us?" he asked. He'd never been part of an "us" before and there was a part of his soul that longed for her answer to be yes. But there was another part—a darker part that knew yes wasn't the answer he was meant to hear.

"I think there could be, but you're going to have to trust me."

"I don't trust easily, Sarah."

"Maybe you haven't met the right person yet."

"Could be."

''I think I'm right. And I'm going to teach you all I know about trust.''

He thought about it. Thought about the incredible ecstasy he'd experienced in her arms and about the longings she'd awakened in him. He should just say no. But he was only a man and the promise in her eyes made him believe that he could manage this.

Harris avoided Sarah and her little house as much as he could over the next few days. Though her family called to him in a way nothing other than high finance ever had. He'd taken on a new consulting job in Tokyo as soon as this one in Orlando ended. If nothing else it would give him a good reason to leave.

Halloween was on Thursday and then he'd only have a short stretch of time before Thanksgiving. He hated that holiday the most. Every year he'd watched that damned Macy's parade from his father's penthouse. So close to all those happy laughing families and so damned far away. Harris had a strict policy of being out of the country for all Holidays. This year would be no exception.

He'd stay busy like he always did. And this year he'd keep his distance from Sarah, her restaurant and the family that she kept trying to make him a part of. To keep from remembering what it was like to hold Sarah in his arms and to dream for a moment of something that could never be.

Ray had cajoled him into going to Sarah's restaurant twice but Harris refused to go inside both times. Instead he'd been on the phone with Marshall Turner and the New Deal Developing Consortium who was purchasing Sarah's rental property. Every time his conscience brought up that fact—that Taste of Home would be affected by this takeover—he quieted it. Business and personal lives didn't mix.

He wasn't sure what the next steps were in his relationship with Sarah. Only knew that spending time with her made him ache in a way that couldn't be good.

He wanted her in his bed again. He wanted to exorcise the demon that she'd become to his soul. He wanted to let this obsession run its path so he could be free of it and get on with his normal life. But he didn't want to burden her with his reality. To shatter more of her illusions of what life could be.

And any woman looking for Mr. Right believed in the kind of fairy tales that weren't possible in the real world. A life that didn't involve caring and the emotions that kept roiling through him. But that showed no sign of happening. Because Harris had realized that sex with Sarah was different from sex with other women. It wasn't even sex per se, it was more like making love.

Ray stopped for the third night in front of Taste of Home. Since it was after ten, Harris suspected it wasn't for dinner. Harris had deliberately worked late so that he wouldn't be tempted to see Sarah.

"Why are we here?" Harris asked Ray.

"Sarah's car is back in the shop. I told her we'd pick her up."

"Next time consult me first." This is what came from letting staff eat a meal with you, Harris thought.

"Yes, sir." Ray had stopped being jovial after the first time Harris had refused to go to Sarah's house.

"Ray, you take your job too seriously. I'm paying you to chauffeur me to and from meetings. Not to drive me through life."

"You need someone to," Ray said.

"Not you."

"Hell. Definitely not me. Sarah. She can bring you things no one else can."

"What are you talking about, Ray?" Harris asked. He wasn't sure but his driver seemed almost desperate to get him to see Sarah again.

"*Merda.* I'm trying to help you and Sarah...."

"Don't. I'm not the right guy for her. Surely you can see that."

"Yeah, I know what you are saying, man. But let me tell you letting her go will haunt you."

"I'm already haunted, Ray."

"It gets worse."

"Maybe that's a man's burden."

"Yeah, maybe," Ray said.

He wondered if Ray wasn't having his own woman problems. Ray had the hounded look that only a woman can produce in a man.

"Here she comes."

Ray got out of the car and opened the door for Sarah. She started to slide in, noticed Harris and paused. Damn, she looked better than he'd remembered. He wanted to grab her hand and pull her into the car with him.

To take her in his arms and kiss her until they both forgot about the other problems between them. Problems which stemmed solely from him. Problems that had nothing to do with heat or desire.

"I didn't realize you'd be here," she said.

"It is my car."

"I know. It's just that I had the impression you were avoiding me."

"What are we, in junior high?"

She flushed. "Sarcasm doesn't suit you."

He felt ashamed of himself. "Come on in. I won't bite."

"Biting would be the least of your offenses," she said.

"Suit yourself."

"I will," she said.

She clamored into the car over his legs and sprawled on the seat across from him. She smelled uniquely of Sarah and also of lasagna. He realized he was hungry not for food but for Sarah. His own actions had put a wall between them that only he could tear down.

She was silent while the car rolled through the busy October night. Finally she sighed and looked over at him. "I thought you were going to give us a try."

"I...can't."

She scooted next to him on the seat. The fragrance of her perfume wrapped around him and he clenched his hands to keep from reaching out and touching her.

The way he wanted to. The way he needed to. The way he longed to.

Sweat broke out on the back of his neck. He didn't know if he could do it. Was it already too late to keep her out of his system? Hell, yes his body said. Give up the fight and grab her before she disappeared like every other woman in his life ever had.

She put her hand on his thigh and looked up at him with those dark eyes that promised redemption. Like a hungry man he wanted to reach out and take a chance. But like an alcoholic who'd fallen off the wagon more than once, his cynical side warned she was too good to be true.

"I'm not going to keep throwing myself at you. If you don't want to see me, then stop coming by my restaurant."

"It's not that I don't want to see you, Sarah. It's that you are worlds too soft for a man like me. If you were any other type of woman I'd say to hell with it."

"What type of woman am I?"

"The kind that still believes life is more than a rat race."

"Then let me show you my reality."

"I don't want to have to spend my life trying to find something that doesn't exist."

"Because of your dad?"

Harris shrugged. Sarah slid her arm around his back and leaned her head on his shoulder. "I'm living proof that it exists. Give it a chance."

"How?"

"Come to the Halloween party we're throwing at Taste of Home. Costumes are required."

"I've never put on a costume."

"It'll be fun."

Fun? It would be torture. He'd be surrounded by her warmth, her scent, the essence of this woman and it was impossible to say no to her. So he nodded. At least they'd be in public.

Seven

Witches and bats swung from the ceiling. A kettle filled with dry ice steamed near the register and Burt, dressed like a goblin with an ax in his head and bloodied T-shirt, slumped on the bench near the candy bowl, ''waking'' up to scare kids when they reached for a treat.

Isabella, who was in the drama club at school, wore her costume from last year's production of Romeo and Juliet. All of the wait-staff were in costume, too. Since Sarah was serving as a hostess this evening she'd decided on Elvira Mistress of the Night. With a little help from the WonderBra she thought she looked dang good.

Taste of Home was crowded, Sarah thought with glee. Finally it seemed her restaurant was making a swing toward being more profitable. She'd hired a band for the evening, a group of kids from the high school. They played popular music and golden oldies, which pleased everyone in the crowd.

The only thing missing was Harris. She wasn't sure he was really going to show. Sure he'd said he'd come but she knew this type of party wasn't in his comfort zone. She'd thought about calling and reminding him he'd promised to come tonight but she didn't. She wasn't running after him. If he was interested in her, he had to meet her halfway.

The door opened and a blast of chilly air swept inside. As always the temperature dipped on All Hallows Eve and tonight it was in the low sixties. Not cold for other parts of the country, but for this Florida girl the weather was definitely chilly.

She glanced up and saw Harris. *No costume.* His briefcase in one hand, a bouquet of autumn colored flowers in the other. She felt a rush of pleasure that scared her.

Seeing him shouldn't make her this happy. She shouldn't put so much emotion into this relationship. He'd be gone by Thanksgiving. But she couldn't stop herself. She hurried to his side.

"These are for you," he said.

No one had ever brought her flowers. It was such a small thing but it touched her deeply. She buried her face in them, inhaling deeply. Hiding until she thought she had her emotions under control.

"Thanks."

"I'll take over hosting duties, while you put those in water," Burt said.

Sarah nodded and made her way back to her office. But she didn't have a vase.

"Why don't you put them in the refrigerator until you go home?" Harris suggested.

"Good idea. Are you hungry?"

He gave her the once-over and she flushed as his eyes narrowed in a way she recognized. He whistled softly through his teeth. "For you."

He was eyeing her breasts and she fought the urge to cover her cleavage. "I'm not on the menu."

"You should be."

"Really? You'd share me with others."

"Never," he said, his eyes narrowing.

She wanted to ask if he really meant it but didn't. She was trying to ease him into the world of the living not overwhelm him. But she cherished his words and tucked them away to examine later.

"Did you have dinner?"

"There wasn't any time."

"I'll bring you a plate. Have a seat."

She put the flowers in the refrigerator and fixed Harris a plate of food. She grabbed a basket of bread and a bottle of Merlot. It took several trips to get everything she wanted but soon they were sitting on her office floor on a picnic blanket. While Harris ate dinner Sarah tried to keep the conversation going but she wasn't sure what to say. Their relationship was so tenuous.

"I read that Nick Hornby book. You were right, it was really good."

"I usually am right," she said, winking at him.

"You are? Other than the book name one time," he said.

"I knew you'd enjoy yourself if you came here tonight."

"I must bow to your abilities as a seer."

"There's no magic to my gift. You're easy to read."

"No mystery, huh?"

"Some things about you I'll never understand but books and dinner, well those are easy to predict."

He reached out and caressed her face. "Don't try so hard to understand me. I'm just a man."

"You are much more than that," she whispered.

He leaned forward, brushing his mouth over hers. She let him nuzzle her lips and caress her face. Aware that once again he used passion to distract her. But tonight, with the spirit of Halloween in the air, she didn't mind.

A knock on the door drew them apart. Harris picked up his wineglass and took a sip while she answered the door. "We need you out front. It's time for the costume contest judging.

"I'll be right there," Sarah said.

She straightened her wig and then glanced over her shoulder at Harris. "Coming? We could use one more judge."

He got to his feet in one movement. "Go ahead. I'll clean this up and join you."

She nodded and left Harris in her office. Whenever she tried to include him he always backed away. That's okay, she thought. She would make him part of her community. She'd just keep trying.

Harris drove Sarah's car through the deserted streets of Orlando. Burt and Isabella had taken the limo to a party at Universal Studios so he and Sarah were alone. He'd managed to avoid the costume contest by making some business calls from Sarah's office. He didn't think she'd noticed his absence.

But he'd felt it in his soul. There was a part of him—the lonely child who'd watched other kids in normal households go trick-or-treating—that had wanted to join in Sarah's party. But joining in, putting down roots wasn't for him.

Sarah fiddled with the radio station. Her car stereo was standard issue and the speakers weren't very good. He made a mental note to have a new stereo system installed in her car before he left.

She settled on a jazz station playing Miles Davis. Harris let the trumpet riffs settle over him and tried to pretend this was like any other night. But it wasn't. No night with Sarah was like any other and no one knew that better than he did.

He pulled into her driveway and shut off the car. But made no move to get out. He wanted to go inside her house and make love to her. He wanted to hold her in his arms all night and wake them both up in the morning by sliding into her body. He wanted…

more than just sex for the first time and that made him hesitate.

Sarah opened her door but didn't get out when he made no move to join her. "What's the matter?"

"I don't want to give you the wrong impression," he said. He'd made a decision tonight watching Sarah in her element. A decision to ensure that she didn't change because of him. He didn't want to leave her with his cynicism.

Because there was something pure about her and her outlook on life. Something he'd never really had when he looked at life. And he wanted to preserve that. His world needed more people like Sarah.

"About what?" she asked, she'd removed the El-vira wig. Her normal bouncy hair was a little flatter than usual, still curling around her face.

"Us," he said.

She closed the door, leaning back in her seat. Crossing her arms under her breasts, she shifted slightly in the seat to face him. He knew she was trying to look serious. But she didn't come close.

"I've already been warned. You're leaving in a few more weeks."

Why had he started this conversation? He slid his arm along the back of her seat and rested his hand on her shoulder. He rubbed his forefinger on the edge of the material at her neck, making teasing forays toward the flesh that beckoned him.

"I thought you wanted to talk," she said, shivering under his touch.

No woman had ever reacted as quickly to his caresses the way Sarah did. Physically she was made to be his match. They were so attuned sexually it was eerie, but he didn't dwell on that.

"You distracted me."

"Please. I'm not a sex pot," she said.

How could she affect him so deeply and not be aware of it?

"Woman, you are a living, breathing temptation. I can't be near you and not want you."

She quirked her head to the side. "Is that true?"

"I don't lie," he said, slipping his finger a bit farther down her chest. She trembled and shifted on the seat. Her arms falling to her sides.

"I'm coming to believe that," she said. One of her hands falling to his thigh and kneading it. "What are we doing in the car?"

"I was trying to make sure you understood something," Harris said.

"What?" she asked. Her voice was husky. Her skin flushed and her pupils dilated. She was aroused and watching the change come over her body tightened him painfully. He leaned forward and brushed his lips against the globes of her breasts. Hmm, she smelled so sweet. He ached to possess her again.

Why had he hesitated? Then he remembered. Hurting Sarah wasn't something he could live with. Lifting his head, he stared into her dark eyes.

"You make me want to be better than I am, yet I don't think I can be."

"Stop worrying about me. If my parents' death

taught me one thing it was not to look ahead. That the only time we have is now.''

"All you want is now?" he asked.

She took his face in both of her hands and kissed him thoroughly. Everything he'd come to expect from Sarah was in that kiss. Her sweet caring, her spicy personality and a deep need that he couldn't explain. "I'm hoping I can convince you that we deserve more than that.''

"How are you going to do that?" he asked.

"By showing you what you're missing," she said with a sweet smile that cut him to the bone.

"Don't let me hurt you, Sarah. I don't think I could live with myself if I knew I took the smile from your eyes.''

"I control my happiness, not you,'' she said.

"Hold that thought, honey.''

"I will.''

Harris pocketed her keys and exited the car. Sarah had already climbed out by the time he got there. He took her elbow and led her to the house. "Tonight I'm going to make you think that happiness is a place that belongs to only the two of us.''

One week later, Sarah was alone in her office. The crowd tonight was slow and steady, leaving her too much time to think. Sade sang softly in the background. Her haunting voice singing of *cherishing the day* and Sarah wished that she could do that. But instead she looked to the future and worried. Paul had been easy to love and easy to break her heart over because she'd been young and unaware of the nuances of love.

Harris was different. There was something about him that made her weary and afraid for the first time that she might fall in love with him. It didn't help that Thanksgiving was right around the corner. The family holiday always made her heart feel heavier with the loss of her parents and the loneliness of her life.

Harris was everything she ever wanted in a man. He was a skilled lover who could bring her to the heights of passion again and again each night. She hardly recognized the woman she'd become in bed with him. But she knew that it was a part of herself she'd always hidden because she'd been afraid to risk too much of herself. But with Harris knowing him as she did, she realized it was going to take everything she had to give to keep him in her life. And she realized she wanted—no needed to keep him in her life.

He was also intelligent in ways she hadn't expected him to be. He knew everything. Literally there wasn't a subject that she brought up that he couldn't discuss or argue. She loved listening to him talk about his travels and his studies. Harris was an observer she realized and she wanted to change that.

She could pretend all she wanted that he might stay with her in her little house in Orlando but she knew he'd be leaving two days after Thanksgiving. Not to return to his home in California but to Tokyo. And a small-time restaurateur was no match for the global mover and shaker that Harris was.

She reached for the Magic 8 ball on her desk and flipped it over in her hands. She wasn't going to ask it anything. It wasn't as if the stupid child's toy had any real fortune-telling powers. Yet she asked the one question that had made it difficult for her to sleep in Harris's arms at night.

Will he break my heart? She couldn't even ask it aloud. She had to whisper it in her mind.

Concentrate and ask again.

She threw the ball toward the back of her desk. It rolled off and wedged between the wall and the corner of the desk. Not quite to the floor. Oh, no. This couldn't be a good sign.

She hitched her skirt up around her hips and leaned forward to try to reach the ball and couldn't. Desperation raced through her leaving a lingering unease in the pit of her stomach. She had to ask again.

Or did she? When had she become so hopeless? She knew better than to wait on magic to make things happen in her life. She stood up and marched out of the restaurant. Roger Hammond her night manager was on duty.

She climbed in her car and called Harris's cell phone. She didn't put the car in gear. She couldn't talk and drive without hurting herself or someone else. He answered on the first ring.

"Davidson."

A small tingle went through her when she heard his voice. Though he was shy about relationships and emotion, Harris held nothing back when it came to lovemaking. She'd grown in sensual experience so much in the last two weeks. But she thought now it was time for her to teach him a thing or two. "It's me."

"Hey, you. What's up?" he asked.

"I need to see you."

She heard papers rustle and the squeak of his office chair. She imagined him disheveled, tie loosened, hair rumpled from running his fingers through it. She wished she was in his office with him. She'd rub his shoulders and then offer him a more intimate kind of massage.

"I should be done in an hour. Should I meet you at your place?"

Not tonight. Tonight she was leaving the old ordinary Sarah behind. And she couldn't do that in her homey little bedroom. "Um...no. I'll meet you at your hotel."

"Is everything okay?" he asked. No more rattling papers or chairs. She had his full attention and it made her feel good, almost...cherished.

"Yes. I want to surprise you."

"And you can't do that with your family around?"

"No. Not when I'm planning to seduce my guy."

"Ah, hell. I wish you wouldn't have said that."

"Why?" she asked, pitching her voice in a low sexy whisper. Harris had told her he loved the way her voice sounded first thing in the morning.

"I *have to* stay at work."

For the first time since they'd met she sensed he regretted his job. She took heart from the fact that she was becoming as important to him as work. "Maybe you'll work faster."

"Damn straight, I will."

Silence buzzed on the line and in the background she heard him working on the keyboard. "I should let you go."

"Yeah, I'll see you at my hotel."

"Bye."

"Sarah?"

"Yes?"

"Am I really your guy?" he asked. There was that hint of vulnerability in his voice again. She wanted to cuddle him and assure him but knew only he could decide if he wanted to be her guy.

"Of course you are."

"I've never had this before."

"Had what?"

He hesitated so long she was afraid he wasn't going to answer. "A relationship."

"Well get used to it."

"That's exactly what I'm afraid to do."

"I'm not going to let you get away that easily."

"I'm starting to believe you, you know," he said, quietly.

"Good," she said. He sounded so vulnerable some times she forgot he was a big Norse god of a man who wasn't awed by anything.

"What time is Ray picking you up?"

"In an hour."

"Make it an hour and a half. And I need a favor,"

she said, making plans in her head while she talked to Harris.

"What's in it for me?" he asked.

"You'll have to wait and see."

"What's the favor?"

"Arrange for me to pick up a key to your suite."

"Done."

"What, no more questions?"

"I trust you," he said.

"Do you really?"

"On this I do."

She was hurt but she understood. She knew Harris well enough to comprehend that it was going to take more than a few weeks to win his trust. But she had a bigger goal in mind. She wanted to win his love.

"Knock first," she said at last.

"Sarah…"

"Don't say anything else. We both know where we stand."

"I'm sorry."

"Don't be. I'm planning to change your mind," she said, hanging up the phone.

Eight

I'm planning to change your mind. The words echoed in his head much the same as his father's philosophy did—*love bites*. The buy out of the strip mall was almost complete. Harris rubbed the back of his neck. He'd be all done with this project two weeks early if all went according to plan.

Which didn't surprise him because he'd pushed harder than ever to get everything complete. He wanted no reason to stay in Orlando. No reason to spend more time at Sarah's small house that was beginning to feel like home. The one he'd forgotten he wanted. One that had nothing to do with priceless Chagalls on the wall or Waterford crystal on the table. One that had to do with an emptiness deep inside that a place had never been able to fill before.

Thanksgiving loomed around the corner and he shivered internally at the thought of the holiday. He hated the holiday season. Which is why he spent so much time in Asia. They didn't celebrate the American ones and luckily Harris had no memories of the ones in Asia. So they were an excuse to party.

But he always felt alone. Loneliness was its own sort of comfort for him. Or had been before he'd met Sarah. Now he couldn't fathom spending Spring Festival of the Chinese New Year in Beijing by himself watching the fireworks from his solitary hotel room. But spending it with a woman other than Sarah sounded even less appealing. *Damn.* This was exactly why he'd avoided personal bonds.

He loosened his tie as he entered the hotel and walked toward the elevators. Around him teemed families all sunburned and tired-looking from spending their days at Disney World. Personally Harris had never understood the concept of a vacation where exhaustion was the main goal. He vacationed twice a year in the South Pacific on a very remote island with no phones, faxes or computer modems.

He got off the elevator on his floor and his footsteps slowed. Sarah scared him in ways he'd never thought he could be scared. There was a certain comfort in being a machine. Working all the time and not really interacting socially with other people. Because his control was complete. But with Sarah—he wasn't in control.

He doubted he'd ever be in control where she was

concerned and that made him want to go down to the bar and call her and tell her to go home.

But he'd learned a long time ago that hiding was worse than facing his fears so he continued down the hall. He'd been trying to keep a wall between them. He realized Sarah wasn't going to tolerate that anymore.

Inserting his keycard into the door he opened it and stepped inside. The room was dark. He'd expected the trappings of romance from the woman who believed in love. He'd expected rose petals on the floor and candles on every surface.

Instead he found Sarah sitting on the couch staring out at the sky filled with fireworks. Filled with the illusion that people used to escape the reality of every day. He dropped his brief case. The cloak of guilt draped over his shoulders. He'd done this to her. He'd taken a girl who believed in white knights and happily ever after and brought her to this the cold loneliness that was his life.

His reality. The reality of the Davidson men. Love was a cold and lonely place to be. It didn't even matter if she loved him or not. He knew she cared and caring had cost her dearly.

Dave Matthews Band played from the CD player and Sarah took a sip from a wineglass. He watched her quietly for a few minutes not knowing what to say. His mind was chaos, a turmoil he hadn't been able to quiet since meeting her. A thousand different scenarios spun in his mind and he knew if he could just sort them out a solution would present itself. But there was a desperation inside him toward her. And he thought maybe this was what his father experienced with each new love affair.

"Sarah?" he called, tired of hiding even if it was only from himself.

She shifted on the sofa and stood. There were only shadows in the room. Brief flashes of illuminating light and he knew he should feel better that he couldn't see deadened emotions in her eyes but he didn't. The Sarah he'd come to know deserved a man who was comfortable in the full light of her affection. Not someone who ran from it. Not a man who hid from it and from her.

He crossed the room carefully. He didn't know how to offer comfort. But he'd try. He'd offer to hold her and to help her sort out whatever was troubling her. And if he was the problem, then dammit, he'd leave and let her get on with her life.

"Stop," she said. Her naturally deep voice, husky.

He froze in his tracks. But she said nothing. Took another sip from her wineglass.

"I helped myself to a glass of wine. I hope you don't mind."

"I don't. I'm later than I planned to be."

"That's okay. I chickened out."

He raised one eyebrow at her in question and then realized she couldn't see him. "How?"

"I was trying to be more like the women you usually sleep with, but I...I'm sorry."

"About what?"

"This whole seduction thing. I tried, really I did. But it felt weird."

"What's weird about you and me?" he asked. He walked closer to her. He needed to touch her. To hold her. If he made the wrong step now, she'd be gone. And he needed her to stay. Needed her to never leave and he wasn't sure he had the right to ask her to stay. Even if only for this night.

"Nothing. It just felt like I was trying to be someone else."

"Don't do that," he said. He stopped when a few inches separated them. Her floral fragrance surrounded him, enraging his senses. He covered her lips. They trembled under his fingers. He caressed her, rubbing his thumb against her bottom lip until she turned her head and dropped a kiss in the center of his palm.

"Do you want me?" he asked.

"Yes," she said.

"Then take me to bed and have your wicked way with me."

She laughed and his heart felt lighter. He refused to think any more tonight. Tonight was about Sarah and her needs. This was the one place where he felt qualified to take care of her. Bending, he scooped her up in his arms and started for the bedroom.

"I thought I was in charge."

Now he could see the sparkle in her eyes. He bent and dropped a quick kiss on her lips. "You are. I just felt like being your white knight."

"Oh, Harris. You always are."

She cupped the side of his face, her fingers rubbing over his stubble and Harris wondered if he should shave for her. To make sure he didn't leave a mark on her. But then he realized he wanted to mark her in every way he could. To somehow let the world know that she was his. The thought staggered him but he didn't stop. He forced it to the back of his mind.

Sarah could never be his, he reminded himself.

"Only in your eyes," he said when he could speak.

"Aren't mine the only ones that matter?"

"Tonight they are," he said, bending to take her mouth in his. It felt like a lifetime since he'd tasted her. Since he'd drunk from her until his blood pounded heavily in his veins and his erection strained against his inseam. It felt like a lifetime since he'd caressed her soft skin and tickled the sensitive place behind her ear.

It felt like a lifetime since he'd been home and like a man afraid to believe in tomorrow he ignored that feeling and made love to Sarah. Forcing emotion and rational thought to the background, he vowed to make her his so completely that she'd never forget him when he was gone.

"Put me down," she said as soon as they entered the bedroom. He did, trailing his mouth down her neck and biting her at the place where her pulse beat. It felt like ages since she'd been in his arms. Since their naked skin had pressed against each other. Since she'd experienced the only intimacy she'd been able to get from Harris.

There were no areas on her body that hadn't been explored but tonight she wanted to explore Harris. To lay claim to his body and hopefully a little of his soul.

He was so close his heat wrapped around her and she leaned in resting her head on his chest. His heartbeat was strong and steady. She listened to it for a few beats before she realized how much she wanted this man. The feelings overwhelmed her and she stood on tiptoe, pulling his head down to hers.

Their eyes met and his gaze shifted before he lowered his head those last few inches and took her mouth. There was nothing subtle about Harris. Especially in the bedroom. She pulled free though it would be so easy to let him take control again. Now that Harris was here her confidence was back and she wanted to make love to him.

''Wait for me on the bed,'' she said.

''Okay.''

She entered the bathroom and dressed quickly. The supple feel of the leather bustier and panties was surprising against her flesh. She was already aroused in a way that only Harris had ever made her feel. There was something about the man that touched the woman she hid deep inside.

Tonight she wanted to touch the man deep inside him. And she smiled to herself in the mirror. This outfit ought to help. She bent at the waist and fluffed her hair with her hands. She stood and glanced again at her reflection. She pulled her smudge-free lipstick from her makeup bag and applied a generous coat to her lips. Running her hands down her sides she realized she didn't feel self-conscious in the least.

Opening the door, she peeked out into the room. Harris was lounging on the bed, the comforter and sheets tossed back. He wore only his white cotton briefs. It amazed her that this man was her lover. He should be with some glam-girl who looked liked she belonged in this luxurious suite.

She tugged the top of the bustier up one more time and bit her lip. Since there wasn't a glam-girl to be found, she was going to have to be his mate. Her heart beat a little quicker. Yes, she'd be his mate. In life and love, she decided. Now to convince him.

It's hard to defeat an enemy with outpost in your head. She repeated her favorite Sally Kempton quote in her head as she opened the door completely. She felt vulnerable and exposed. If he didn't care about her the way she cared about him, she was taking a huge risk.

He'd left the bedside light on and the rest of the room was in shadows. His chest and abs were strongly delineated and her fingers tingled with the need to stroke him. Tonight she promised herself she'd take the time to taste every hard inch of his torso. She wanted to see what made him clench and claw with need.

She cleared her throat, wanting his full attention on her as she made her entrance.

"Ready?" she asked.

"Honey, a man doesn't get much more," he said, gesturing to the hard-on straining against his briefs.

The moistness between her legs confirmed what she already knew—she was ready for him, too.

"Good," she said, pushing open the door and stepping into the room. The carpet under her feet felt warm and comforting after the tile. She'd forgotten the stiletto heels.

Harris didn't seem to notice her missing shoes. He bolted up off the bed and came to her in a rush. All thoughts of control disappeared as he swept her up in his arms. His mouth ravished hers. His hands caressed everywhere. His fingers dipping into the demicups of her bustier and tweaking her nipples.

Sensation rushed through her, she had to clutch at his shoulders to support herself. His skin was warm to the touch and she kneaded his shoulders and then skimmed her hands down his back, sliding them beneath his briefs and cupping the cool flesh of his buttocks in both her hands.

Harris tried to push the cups of her bra out of the way but the leather was stiff and formed. Cursing, he reached into one cup and pushed her breast until the nipple peaked over the top of the leather cup. He bent and suckled her. She melted.

His hands roamed over her back, following the line of her thong to her wet hot center. He traced a pattern there between her legs and then slid his finger under the gusset of her panties and touched her.

She moaned his name. He shoved her panties down. Then took two steps to the wall, leaning back against it, he shifted his grip on her and removed his briefs.

"Ride me, Sarah."

She wrapped her legs around his hips and waited for him to take her. He was hard and ready at her entrance but he didn't thrust into her.

"This is your show."

She swallowed, reached between her legs and held him at her entrance, then sank down on him. As always there was that too tight feeling. She waited for her body to adjust to his length and then she tightened the walls of her vagina around him and began to move on him.

She gripped his shoulders and rocked her hips. Harris lowered his head and dropped love kisses on her neck and shoulder, suckling the point where they met. His hands roamed her back, stopping on her buttocks. Cupping them and running his finger along the furrow between her cheeks.

She tightened around him as he caressed her there. Rocking harder against him until everything spun out of control and she climaxed calling his name.

Harris held her until she calmed down. He was still hard between her legs. "You didn't...?"

"Not yet. I want this night to last forever."

He carried her to the bed and dropped her lightly on it. "Roll over."

She did as he ordered. He unfastened the bustier and tossed it aside. The sheet against her sensitive breasts chaffed. Harris's hands roamed over her back, tracing the line of her spine to her buttocks then on to her legs.

He returned again and again tracing the same line

until she was undulating on the bed and ready to scream his name. With each pass his fingers came closer to her center which was empty and aching to be filled again by him.

He leaned over her. Covering her body with his warmth. His breath rasping in her ear. His hands sliding over her sides now, his fingers reaching under her body to caress her nipples and her hipbones.

"Ready for me?" he asked, right in her ear.

"Yes," she said on a moan. Her hips moving against him. His erection brushing between her buttocks and then right over her center.

He shifted against her and she felt him adjust himself before he plunged into her channel from behind. This time he was in charge. He slid one hand under her belly and then down to the center of her desire. Rubbing the little button in a counter rhythm to his thrusts. His other hand he kept on the back of her neck so that she couldn't move. She felt possessed by him. She felt branded by him. And as she felt her climax tightening her lower body at the same time he stiffened and spilled his seed in her she felt as if their souls mingled.

Harris held Sarah close in the aftermath. He held her until he'd stopped shuddering and the sheen of sweat on his back had dried. She just lay there beneath him. And he felt like he could protect her for a little while.

But they couldn't stay like this all night. He'd like to. It gave him an easy excuse to hide from her. He could keep her like this and bring her to the brink again and again. Not give either of them a chance to think or talk.

But that wasn't fair. He rolled over and propped some pillows behind his back. The he tugged Sarah into his arms and told himself holding her like this wasn't protective. Women liked to cuddle after mind-blowing sex. But Harris had never done it before. *Only with Sarah.*

Only for Sarah was he tempted to be better than he knew he could be. Only Sarah made him want to stick around.

Sarah traced random patterns on his chest. She'd wanted to put on a nightshirt but he'd coaxed her into staying nude. He'd never get his fill of just looking at her.

Sated, he felt like he could hold her and not be overwhelmed for a few minutes by the need to possess her. He wasn't sure of his path. He could leave in two days.

His work here was finished but he wanted to stay with Sarah. He knew he shouldn't stay for the next few weeks because he wouldn't stay beyond that. The only reason why he'd become her lover was because he had a definite end date.

He was managing his expectations and managing hers as well. Tonight threw a wrench in his plans. That get-up she'd had on. He thought he'd come in his briefs when he saw her. He'd never imagined her buying and wearing anything so erotic. But she'd looked sweet at the same time. The subtle hesitancy in her steps and the doubt in her eyes.

She deserved a man who could commit to her and her family. Who could commit to giving her the children she dreamed of having. A man who could commit his heart to hers for a lifetime. Not a man like Harris Davidson.

Regret lanced through him and he was tempted to get out of bed. He freaking needed to get out of the bed and put some distance between them. But he'd seen the vulnerability in her earlier and he wasn't going to put that look back in her eyes. *Not now.*

He bent, rubbing his face against her soft curly hair. Inhaling deeply he closed his eyes and filed it away for a time when he'd be alone.

"Will you have time next week to go to the homeless shelter with me?"

"I'm finished with my job on Friday," he said abruptly.

She stiffened her fingernails digging into his chest. He reached up and pried them out of his skin, smoothing her hand against his chest. "I thought you'd be here until Thanksgiving. That's still two weeks away."

"Things went smoother than I'd anticipated."

"Are you leaving?"

"Maybe."

"Would you stay if I asked you to?"

He wasn't sure. He hated being out of control and that's exactly what he was around Sarah. He let the silence build between them. Sarah eased away from him and tugged the sheet up over her body.

He'd done it without even trying. He'd made her feel small and unworthy. He didn't look at her. Refused to see the look he knew he'd put in her eyes.

"When will you know for sure?" she asked, her voice dull, lifeless.

God, he could be a bastard sometimes.

"We're delivering eviction notices to the tenants tomorrow. If there aren't any complications, I should know by Friday."

"What exactly do you do?" she asked.

"I appraise commercial property for retail potential then negotiate a buyout and restructure the property for its maximum retail potential."

"Why do you evict businesses?" she asked.

He didn't want to talk about his job. Didn't want to think about it right now. He was trying to make the most important decision of his life. One that he'd never have been able to make in the past. One that involved this woman, sitting as far from as she could on the king-size bed.

"They're deadweight."

"Deadweight?" she prompted. He knew she wasn't really listening to him.

"Either they aren't the right business for the new image or they aren't maximizing their potential earnings."

"So you just kick them out?"

"I don't want to talk about my job." He shoved his hands in his hair and rubbed his temples. He had the beginnings of a headache. Was this how his father's problems had started? One little ache that he'd used as an excuse to not leave his room.

Harris remembered his dad locked in his bedroom for days on end when Harris was in middle school. Always with a headache. Screw that, Harris thought. He wasn't going to fall prey to whatever weakness drove his father.

He turned Sarah's face toward him. She kept her chin down and he tried to tip it up but she jerked her face away. "Talk to me, Sarah."

"I'm afraid I can't talk about anything else right now."

Harris knew he was going to have to give her something. No, he wasn't. He was going to have to give up something. The thing that he'd been using to protect himself from her. The thing that he'd been clinging to in order to keep himself from being hurt. And that thing was the one thing he'd vowed he'd never give up. His security wall around his emotions. "Honey, please don't shut down on me."

She blinked a bunch of times and sniffled, wrinkling the end of her nose. Knowing she was trying not to cry made him wonder what kind of crud he was. How did a man who spoke six languages fluently not know how to communicate?

"I can't deal with this right now, Harris. I've had a big night. My Magic 8 ball is trapped behind my desk, I bought leather undergarments. I had kinky sex. And...you're leaving."

He tugged her into his arms, wrapped her tight in

his embrace and lowered his head to brush kisses against her hairline. ''I'm sorry.''

''I know you have a hard time with relationships. I know that you think they are all about obsession but I thought I was showing you that life could be different.''

''This isn't really about you,'' he said carefully.

''What?''

''I learned a long time ago that you can't control the way someone else feels.''

''I realize that. I don't think you know how you feel.''

''I know all right. I'm just not sure how to express it.''

''Tell me what you are feeling.''

''Never.''

''Harris, I give up.'' She climbed out of bed. He watched her walking away and he knew that this was it. If he didn't make some changes in his life, he'd never find the elusive dream that woke him sometimes in the middle of the night.

Nine

"Sarah, wait."

She paused but didn't turn around. She was on the verge of tears and she wasn't sure of herself right now. She'd bared her soul to Harris and being the man he was, he didn't even notice.

"Why should I?" she asked. A part of her wanted to shake him. To make him realize what they could have. Because the man who had spent most of November at her house, fitting into her family was one who could be her mate for life.

She heard the rustle of the bedcovers and the tread of his footsteps on the carpet. An instant before his hands touched her shoulders she felt his warmth all along her back. She wanted to lean back against him. To once again wallow in the protected state she'd been in earlier when he'd covered her body and made her feel cherished.

But she didn't give in. Her own illusions had led her to this point and she wasn't believing in the fairy tale any more. Fairy tales were for girls who spent the days looking out the window and waiting to be rescued. She was no man's Cinderella and Harris had just proved it.

"I want to say the words that will make this right for you."

For her? What about making it right for them? She glanced over her shoulder at him. "Make what right? There aren't any magic words I'm waiting to hear from you that will make me feel better."

"Then what do you need from me?" he asked. His confusion was plain. He didn't know what to say to make her feel good. And he'd said it earlier. He couldn't really make her happy. Only she could do that. And she wasn't even sure if she knew how to do it with him. She pivoted to face him.

She'd never seen him look more alone. He stood there naked and proud. A tough guy who needed no one and she saw her chance for a future with him dim.

She knew he wasn't going to cave in and let her see the inside of his soul though that was what she wanted. Because she sensed the tender man under the tough outer shell. The man who needed some softness in his life.

"I don't know. It seems every time I glimpse a part of the real Harris you shut me down and push

me away. I'm not begging you for crumbs anymore.
I deserve better. And so do you.''

He clenched his fists and jaw. She'd never seen him
so angry. Not even when he'd discovered Ray fixing
spaghetti in her house. "No, I don't."

"Why don't you, Harris? Everyone is entitled to
happiness."

"Happiness is a pipe dream. Reality is content-
ment."

"I'm not going to argue semantics with you. We
have a chance for something special here. I know you
feel it."

"I do want you," he said.

"Well if you want me I'm here."

"I do."

"Couldn't prove it by me," she said. She was tired
of letting him trample on her heart. She'd never
wanted to impress a man before. And he didn't even
seem to notice all the things she was doing for him.
Maybe that was her problem, she should be doing
them for herself.

"Want to go back to bed and I will," he said,
reaching for her. His big hand enveloped her shoulder
and tugged her closer to him. She almost gave in but
it felt too wrong now. What had felt supremely deli-
cious earlier now felt…tainted.

"No, thanks, I've got a vibrator at home."

He clenched his fists. She knew she'd gone too far
but he'd hurt her. She'd let him do it and so she was
partially angry with herself.

"Don't ever belittle what we've shared like that again."

"I'm still mad at you, but that comment was rude and I apologize for it."

"Yes it was. I'm more than a stud to you. And you're more than a night's pleasure to me."

"I know," she said. "Which is why I'm leaving. I'm half in love with you and I'm not a masochist."

"Dammit, woman," he said, rubbing his forehead.

"You okay?" she asked.

He closed his eyes and tipped his head back. "I've got a damned headache."

"Do you get them often? You're probably stressed out."

"I'm not *stressed out*. Men don't have that problem."

What did men have? she wondered, but didn't ask. Harris had some strange notions of what was acceptable behavior for men and what wasn't. And there was nothing she could say to change his mind.

"Well, you've been working hard. Maybe you should take a few days off and rest."

"Never," he growled.

"Why not cut yourself some slack?" she asked, sensing she was close to finding the answers to the real trouble between them.

"Because that's how it starts. A little headache, then staying in bed for a few days. Before you know it a month has past and you haven't moved."

"You've done that?" she asked. She couldn't imagine someone as self-disciplined as Harris, lying in bed all day. He'd go crazy after the first hour or so.

"No."

Suddenly she realized where this was leading. "Your dad?"

"Yes."

"Harris, you are not your dad. I think I've said that before."

"You have. I know that. But no one has ever affected me the way you do, Sarah."

"Oh, Harris," she said, her heart breaking for the lonely life he'd lead.

"Don't say my name like that. I don't want pity from you."

As if she'd pity him. He was too self-confident. Too sure of himself to elicit pity from her. "Pity is the last thing I feel for you."

"What do you feel for me?" he asked.

She bit her lip. She wasn't going to bare her soul. "Too much. Which is why I'm leaving now."

"Please don't go," he said. There was something in his voice that made her believe he needed her caring and affection. That made her want to stay and convince him love was real.

"I need more than the hope that someday you'll care about me. We've been down this road before."

"My dad is the reason I can't stay," he said.

That was a cop-out and he knew it. She saw the knowledge in his eyes. She felt achy and vulnerable and didn't want to say something mean again but knew cruel words hovered on the edge of her tongue.

She loved Harris, she realized. It wasn't just a passing fancy or a spicy hot affair but deep affection and a connection that went so deep inside her she knew when he left she'd never be free of him. "Can't or won't?"

"What's the difference?" he asked. She sensed he was stalling for time.

A big part of her understood that he was afraid of turning out like his dad. She could rationalize his behavior but it didn't stop her from wanting to shake him. Make him wake up and see that they had a chance at something really great. Because she'd never connected with another person the way she had with Harris.

"Do you really think you'll lock yourself in my bedroom?" she asked at last.

He raised one eyebrow at her. "Maybe not at first. But you deserve better than a guy who's afraid to let down his guard."

"Do you want to let it down?" she asked.

"Hell, yes." The sincerity in his eyes. The way he reached for her and then dropped his hands convinced her that there was a future for them. She could keep loving him, keep working to convince him that the darker side of love—obsession—wasn't waiting for him.

"That's enough for me, Harris," she said, stepping forward and wrapping her arms around him.

"It shouldn't be. You're so used to working all the time and settling for any attention that you think I'm worth your time."

She struggled to understand what he was saying. Why would he think he wasn't worth her time? She was the one who ran a small failing restaurant. Probably one that Harris would classify has dead weight if he was taking over her strip mall.

"I'm not settling for anything."

"Then ask me again to stay. Really ask me, don't hedge or give yourself a way out."

She took a step closer to him. "Will you stay with me until you have to go to Tokyo? Then when your business brings you back to the States, come here?"

"Yes," he said, the word barely a whisper. Then he lowered his mouth and kissed her. She tried to tell herself that it was only passion she felt in his embrace but she thought it might be tinged with desperation, which worried her.

Sarah's office was too small for his taste but it suited her. She was playing Moby on her CD player and talking on the phone to one of her food distributors. There was nothing the least bit sexual about her at this moment but he was turned on all the same.

Her hair was pulled back at the nape but the image of her last night with her thick curls floating around her shoulders and that naughty leather bustier stayed in his mind. He reached for the clip and unfastened it. Tossing it on her desk, she gave him a look that told him to keep his hands to himself but he shrugged at her.

Taking the thick mass of her hair in his hands, he

combed through it with his fingers until it was once again the way he remembered it.

She swiveled her chair to face the wall. Propping one hip on her desk, he toyed with the hem of her skirt. Slipping his hand up her thigh. She put her hand on top of his stopping the upward movement of his touch. He settled for tracing a pattern on her inner thigh and was rewarded when she shifted restlessly on her chair.

Sarah ended her conversation. "Don't you have anything to do today?"

"Nope. I'm all yours." He felt light in a way he never had before. He didn't want to examine it or delve too deeply into it because he knew that he'd have to pay for feeling this good, but right now that didn't seem to matter.

It was a crisp November day for Florida. Highs in the sixties and the woman he was involved with was smiling at him in a way that made the sun seem dull. He felt for the first time that he was actually in the right place. In a place where he belonged.

"All mine?"

"Yes, ma'am."

She straightened his tie, which he knew was not askew and then smoothed her hands across his shoulders. "Turn around."

"Why?"

"I have a job you might be right for," she said.

He pivoted. She ran her hands over his arms, testing the resilience of his biceps. Unable to help himself, he flexed his muscles. He worked out twice a day usually and this morning he'd coaxed Sarah into joining him in the weight room.

"You should do. I need a studly man like you."

He raised on eyebrow at her. "I aim to please."

Kicking the door to her office shut, he took her in his arms. Lowering his head to hers, he took her mouth the way he wanted to take her body. Quick and deep. She moaned deep in her throat. He slid his hands around to her backside and lifted her more fully into contact with his aching body.

"Stop."

"Why?"

"I'm at work," she said, pushing away from him. She grabbed the hairclip from her desk and bound her hair back up.

"No one will know."

"Everyone will know. I never close my door."

"I thought that's what you wanted."

"I was teasing you. I'm sorry."

"I'm not upset," he said. And he wasn't. There'd be plenty of time to make love to Sarah later.

"I need a favor," she said, opening her office door.

Harris noticed one of the prep chefs watching the door with a smirk on his face. He made a mental note to have a word with the young punk before he left Taste of Home today. Sarah shouldn't have to put up with any teasing from her staff.

Sarah was wringing her hands together. What was making her so nervous?

"You can tease me any time you want," he said, feeling very indulgent where Sarah was concerned.

He dropped a kiss on her forehead to mask his own emotions and turned away. "Now, name your favor."

"Can you help me move my desk?" she asked, after a few minutes had passed.

The room they were in didn't have a lot of space. "This is probably the best place for your desk. You should think about getting a smaller one."

"Thanks for the advice but this is all I can afford. I don't want to move my desk, I dropped something back there and can't reach it."

"What'd you drop?"

She crossed her arms over her chest. "My Magic 8 ball."

"Can't live without that, huh?" he asked, unable to imagine this savvy business woman consulting a child's toy for advice.

"Hold the smart remarks. I noticed you checking your pager every five minutes for stock market updates."

"That's hardly the same thing."

"It's exactly the same thing. You can't change the course of the market but it makes you feel better to watch it."

She made an odd kind of sense. Not that he'd ever share her opinion with any of his colleagues. They'd think he'd gone off the deep end. And maybe he had. Maybe that was why he felt the way he did. "So the Magic 8 ball makes you feel better?"

"Yes."

"Then by all means, let's get it."

"I tried but my arms aren't long enough."

"Where'd you drop it?"

"Back there."

Harris sat on her desk and reached down between the wall and the office furniture but he couldn't grasp it. He grabbed the bottom of her desk and pulled it out from the wall. The black ball dropped to the floor and Sarah scurried under his legs to grab it. Harris waited until she was out from under the desk to shove it back into place.

She shook it glanced at the answer window and set the ball down on her desk.

"What'd you ask it?"

A flush covered her cheeks. She wasn't going to tell him. Intriguing…what could Sarah be unsure about? Suddenly he realized there was probably a lot she wasn't sure of and most of it involved him. But he was feeling good today and didn't dwell on the future.

"Mind if I give it a try?" he asked.

"Be my guest."

He took the ball and asked, "Would Sarah like me to make love to her on her desk?"

It is decidedly so.

He handed the ball to her and watched her flush as he once again closed her office door. Cleared a spot for her on the desk and lifted her up.

"Harris," she said.

"Yes, honey."

"What's gotten into you today?" she asked.

"You."

"Me?"

"Me and you," he said, bending to kiss her tenderly. The feelings she evoked in him were both sweet and savage. He gentled himself. "I'm not going to trust a child's toy. Do you want me?"

"Oh, yes," she said, wrapping her arms around his neck and giving a kiss he'd die remembering.

The knock on her door sounded just as Harris climaxed. She felt the pulses of his completion on the heels of her own. She was shivering and shaking and not sure where they were. Harris cursed savagely under his breath. Pulled out of her body leaving her feeling empty and alone and zipped his pants.

"Just a minute," Sarah called. "Oh my God. I knew we shouldn't do this here."

Harris calmly smoothed her skirt down and brushed his lips over hers. "Calm down. You look fine."

"I don't feel fine." She was a bundle of nerves and fire. Confident that she'd found a lover who understood her and who was more than her match—she realized her power as a woman.

"You don't?" he asked, teasing her with a look that made her want to throw him on the desk and ravish him.

"No, I feel like a live wire. Is my hair all in the clip?"

"Yes. But your shirt isn't buttoned properly."

She quickly fixed her buttons. This had never happened to her before. If it had been any other man but Harris she would have been embarrassed. But Harris had changed since their conversation last night and she felt like finally they were heading toward a real relationship.

He'd said he'd stay with her and it wasn't business holding him in Florida. But their relationship. A little more time, she thought, was all she needed to convince him that forever wasn't a bad thing.

Everything was just about perfect, which should worry her. That always meant something big was coming. Something was going to happen. But not today, she thought.

Roger was waiting for her when she opened the door. He smiled apologetically. "This just came."

She opened the envelope Roger handed to her with shaking hands. The return address was The New Deal Developers. She had a sinking feeling before she looked at the note.

"Let's hope the rent isn't too steep," she said.

"Whatever it is, we'll figure out how to make it work," Roger said.

She scanned the letter—twice before the words sank in. How could this be? It wasn't a rent increase but an eviction notice. She felt her stomach sink and she thought for a minute she might throw up. Oh, God. How was she going to keep her parents' dream alive without the restaurant?

"Sarah, is everything okay?" Harris asked, wrapping his big arm around her shoulders and offering her comfort. She felt reassured with him by her side. He wasn't Paul. He wasn't going to leave her when things got rough.

His business might call him away but a part of her

believed he'd come back to her. Home to her. And that was just as important to her as keeping her parents' dream alive.

"No. Nothing is okay. Can you believe this? We're being evicted. They don't give us much time. Just two weeks."

"Those are the terms of the lease?" Roger asked.

"Yes. They are. I can't believe this. I'm so angry."

"Me, too," Roger said. "We're going to need to talk to the employees soon. The whole mall is abuzz with the news. It'd be better if they hear it from you."

"Okay. I'm going to call the developer and get all the details. Call everyone in for a two o'clock meeting."

Roger left and Harris said nothing. "Do you think you could help me out here?"

"No," he said, quietly.

"Why not?" she asked. She had that odd sinking feeling in her stomach. She knew that Harris had told her last night about evictions and buyouts but surely he didn't have anything to do with this one. Surely he would have said something to her if he did.

"It would be a conflict of interest," he said.

She knew even though he didn't say the words. She needed to hear it. She needed some proof that the man she'd been falling in love with didn't care enough to tell her she was losing her business. "Because we're involved, right?"

"No. Not because we're having an affair. I helped New Deal negotiate their buyout."

Sarah tried to hold onto her temper. She knew that

Harris didn't really understand what went into a healthy relationship. She knew that he battled the past and what he knew of love each time he took her in his arms. But that didn't matter. One time she wanted to be involved with a guy who she could count on when the chips were down. "What? Why didn't you say anything to me?"

"Business is confidential."

"Business? We don't have business between us."

"That's exactly my point."

"This stinks. You don't trust me at all. I thought we were building toward something lasting."

"We are. New Deal has nothing to do with us. You couldn't afford the rent even if they'd let you stay. Your profits aren't high enough to make you competitive with the other companies that are coming in here."

"Am I deadweight, Harris?"

"Stop making it personal. You, Sarah Malcolm, aren't deadweight. However, Taste of Home is."

"There's no way to make this not personal. I am Taste of Home. And I thought you were part of my family. I invited you into my home. I showed you what loving another person can mean and…"

Harris came closer to her. He reached out to take her in his arms and she flinched away. She was beyond angry and the thought of Harris touching her was abhorrent right now. "You are more than this restaurant. It's not even your dream."

"My dreams? Please don't try to tell me this is about my dreams."

"I'm only pointing out facts. If you'd calm down you'd see this is a blessing in disguise."

"All I see is the last connection I have to my parents is gone."

"It is not. You have your memories and your siblings. That's far more concrete than this building."

"Please tell me the man who has no human connections isn't telling me that family means more than anything else," she said. The Harris she'd come to know would always put his business in front of personal relationships. He'd just proved it.

"Just because I don't have what you do doesn't mean I don't recognize its worth."

"I wish I could believe that," she said, as reality began to creep into the happily-ever-after tapestry she'd been weaving in her head for her and Harris.

"Why can't you?" he asked. He reached for her but she shrugged away.

She didn't want him touching her. Not now when she still felt vulnerable and betrayed. "Because contrary to my recent behavior, I'm not stupid."

He let his hand drop back to his side. "I never thought you were stupid."

"Just convenient," she said, thinking about how easily she'd gone to him. She'd wanted to believe that he could be her forever man. She wanted to believe that after all those years of being alone and lighting candles for a man to come into her life that finally the right one had.

"Not particularly. You've made me uncomfortable since the moment we met."

Somehow that didn't reassure her. She wanted to hear words of love from him. She wanted an apology. She wanted something that she realized Harris was incapable of giving her. For the first time she understood their relationship from his perspective. "I guess I really was just a vacation fling."

"How can you say that? I've given you more of myself than any other woman." He shoved his hands through his hair.

"I'm flattered, really, I am."

"Sarcasm doesn't become you."

"It's either this or losing my temper," she said. Remembering her rude comments from last night she knew she'd better keep hold of her temper.

"Go ahead. I can handle it." He closed the space between them, lowering his hands to her shoulders.

She shivered under his touch. Was it only a few minutes ago that everything had felt so right?

"I can't," she said. She needed to get away from him. She pivoted around to face her desk. She remembered Harris sliding into her on the desk. Remembered the completeness she'd felt and the sense of rightness. More fool she.

"What was that earlier? One last quickie before you leave town?"

"I told you I'd come back," he said.

"Sorry if I don't believe you," she said.

"Don't do that. What we have…I can't describe it. I wouldn't have stayed for anyone else."

"Later when I'm not angry I might feel good about

what you are saying. But right now all I feel is betrayed. I trusted you, Harris."

"I'm not in the wrong here, Sarah. When you calm down enough I think you'll see that," he said. He leaned against her desk, crossing his arms over his chest.

He sounded so calm and controlled and she felt like she was about to explode. A million different feelings roiled around inside her and she wasn't sure which way to turn. "Harris, there isn't enough time in eternity to make me forgive what you've done."

"I don't see why this changes anything."

"Then you're not the man I thought you were," she said softly. "Please leave."

"Okay. Can I see you tonight?" he asked.

"No, Harris."

"This is it, isn't it?" he asked.

There was coldness in her eyes now that surprised her. She nodded and looked away. Couldn't look at him now when she had too much to deal with. She didn't even want to think about her heart breaking.

"You said you loved me earlier, did you mean it?" he asked.

She didn't want to remember her words. Just once she wanted to be the strong one. Instead of the needy one but it was too late. Too late to call back the words, too late to protect herself.

"Yes," she said softly.

"Isn't that reason enough to try to work this out?" he asked.

She wished it were. But she didn't see how it could

ever work between them unless he loved her. And she refused to ask him how he felt about her.

"There is no way to work this out…unless you could talk to The New Deal people," she said.

"I won't," he said, shoving his hands into his pockets.

Wrapping her arms around her waist, she said, "Then I guess it's over."

"I knew it," he said.

"Knew what?" she asked, not sure where he was going.

"That love wasn't all softness and light."

"Don't bring cynicism into this," she said.

"Why not, you brought manipulation in?" he asked.

"How did I manipulate you?" she asked.

"When you asked me to negotiate with the developers. Because I won't do that I don't measure up in your eyes and now you don't love me. Someone once told me that love wasn't like that," he said.

She was a bit ashamed of herself but she hadn't meant to manipulate him. "It's not the same. My loving you doesn't depend on your actions toward my business."

"It sure as hell feels like it."

"Then you're missing the big picture."

"What is the big picture?" he asked.

She shrugged. "I'm not sure anymore. I thought it was you and me—together. But now I have to wonder if I was just imagining it."

"Well I'd have to say you did a good job of convincing me that all those happily-ever-after tales were worth a shot. I let myself be pulled into your illusion.''

She heard him leave. And the first time since she met Harris she was glad that he ran from involvement.

Ten

Harris knew what he'd found with Sarah wouldn't last so it came as no surprise to find himself outside her restaurant alone. The curse of the Davidson men strikes again, he thought. He turned to leave.

"Hey, man," Burt said. "You up for a little one-on-one basketball tonight?"

Harris wanted to say yes. It would give him an excuse to see Sarah again. And he liked Burt. He liked the kid's smart mouth and intelligence and the way Burt thought that charm could get a man through life. "I think I've worn out my welcome at your house."

"I doubt it," Isabella said. "Sarah's crazy about you."

"Not anymore." He didn't know if she'd ever

thought that. It seemed to him that Sarah had been looking for something elusive with him. Something more than the nights of hot passion they'd shared. More than the quiet conversation and debates about books and movies. More than Harris could give and finally she'd figured that out.

"What's going on?" Burt asked, all humor gone from the young man.

"Taste of Home has been evicted from the mall."

"What does that have to do with you?" Isabella asked. Sarah's sister looked too much like Sarah for Harris's peace of mind. He couldn't look into those dark brown eyes one more time and see disappointment.

"I negotiated the buyout."

"Are you the one evicting us?" Isabella asked again.

Burt cursed under his breath and though Harris longed for a fight he hoped Burt kept his temper under control. Fighting with Sarah's brother was something he wouldn't do.

"In a manner of speaking."

"Stop the corporate double-talk and tell us what's going on," Burt said. He dropped his backpack on the ground and flexed his muscles under the T-shirt. Harris hoped the kid wasn't working up the nerve to punch him.

"I'm a consultant to the group that purchased the strip mall. I analyzed the occupants and recommended they evict the ones that didn't fit with the new image," Harris said, inching out of Burt's range.

"Did you know Taste of Home was our restaurant?" Isabella asked.

"Yes," he said, running his hands through his hair. Words of explanation hovered on his tongue but he left them unsaid. He stunk at personal relationships and now he knew why—they hurt too damned much.

"How could you do that? Our sister loves you."

Did she? She'd said so but then she'd pushed him away. Harris hoped she'd been trying to manipulate him with her emotions but a part of him knew Sarah wasn't an actress.

And that she wouldn't lie about her response to him. But that didn't stop him from hoping she didn't really love him. Because the woman he'd left a few minutes ago looked like her world had changed.

Like the gauze that she used to view life through had been striped away. He didn't want to be responsible for breaking her heart and shattering her illusions. Even though he knew he had.

"It was just business," he said. The Malcolms all needed a course in business realities.

"What about all the time you've spent at our house, didn't it mean anything?" Isabella asked.

"It meant more than any of you can ever understand," Harris said. "When your sister calms down, tell her I never intended to hurt her."

When he got to the limo Ray was on the phone and Harris waved him to stay where he was opening his own door.

Harris entered the car smoothly and shut the door before either of Sarah's siblings could respond. For a minute he was isolated from everyone. The tinted windows ensuring his privacy. The raised partition making sure that he was ensconced in a world he could control.

He thought it would be soothing after the emotional interchanges with the Malcolms but instead the limo felt oddly flat. Stale almost.

Ray lowered the partition. "Where to, Harris?"

Harris cursed under his breath. His first instinct was to go to the hotel, pack his stuff and go back to L.A. There he could spend his time alone in his cold sterile mansion licking his wounds. But that sounded exactly like something his dad would do.

"Just drive," Harris said at last. He'd guarded his heart. He'd protected himself from Sarah. Was she the kind of woman who could make him run and hide from the world?

The deluge of memories dancing in his mind said she was. He remembered the hundred sweet things she did for him. The way she'd made him a part of her life even though he'd struggled to keep her at bay.

He didn't understand why she couldn't see that business and relationships were two different things. Harris had always been good at business and money. But bonds with people had always eluded him. Not just a love affair with one special woman but even the simplest bonds of friendship had always seemed out of his grasp.

He realized suddenly that he was hiding from whatever had hurt his father. Whatever it was that had driven his dad up to his penthouse and not let the man come out.

Affection? Caring? Dependence… He couldn't afford to be dependent on anyone.

''Any ideas where you want to go yet, *compare?*''

''Back to my hotel.''

''You look like a *babbeo* who just got sucker-punched.''

''I feel like one.''

''Sarah?''

''Why are women so hard to understand?''

''I've never been able to figure that out. Give me a punk with knife and I know how to come out a winner. But with the opposite sex? I feel like an idiot, you know like a *gavone.*

Harris shrugged. He didn't want to discuss his inadequacies.

''How bad is this problem?'' Ray asked.

He rubbed the back of his neck and glanced out the window. ''She's angry.''

''Will an expensive gift fix it?'' Ray asked.

Harris wasn't sure. He started running the numbers in his head. Making columns of pros and cons. The pluses of fixing things with Sarah were scary. He'd have to let go of the control he'd always used to protect himself. He'd have to change. The downside, the minuses, offered him the comfort of his routine and the continuation of his lonely existence.

''I don't think anything will,'' he said to Ray but

in his mind, he was playing with the puzzle that was Sarah and trying to find a way to get her back without losing his control.

Four hours later, Sarah talked to her staff with her siblings and Roger by her side. She was suddenly the same girl she'd been at eighteen. There was so much work to be done and she was inadequate to the task.

But she'd made everything work then and she'd do it again. She'd go talk to the new developers. She knew they hadn't had a chance to talk to any of the renters. And she knew that Harris wouldn't have mentioned anything about the businesses or hers in particular because he compartmentalized everything.

While she admired his business acumen and later she might understand why he'd acted the way he had, right now the only thing that dominated her mind was that he'd betrayed her. And she'd just gotten used to believing he could be her Prince Charming.

The picture of her parents over the register seemed to stare at her with a certain sense of...disappointment. After keeping it all together for twelve years she was going to fail them. She'd come so close to making their final wish come true. Her siblings were almost out of high school, almost to college and on their own. It seemed wrong to fail so close to the finish line.

"Are we closing down now?" asked one of her waiters, Antonio. He was fifty-five and had worked at the restaurant when her parents owned it. Most of her servers were older and had worked for her for years. In a way the restaurant was the extended family she and the twins didn't have.

"No. We're open today as usual. We'll have another all-staff meeting tomorrow morning."

Why hadn't she been able to show Harris that family wasn't just blood relatives? Family came in all shapes and sizes.

"Phone call for you, Sarah," Roger said.

"I'll take it in my office," she said, fearing it might be more bad news. She smiled at her staff before she left. "We'll get through this. I promise you."

It was strange to walk through the kitchen and see it empty during the day. She remembered her father, a Master Chef at the stoves. Remembered the loving way he'd always prepared every meal before they'd served it.

His premise was to give each customer a little *taste of home*. It had taken her a long time to get used to the kitchen without her dad. She didn't know if she was going to be able to come to terms of being without this restaurant.

She prayed for a miracle as she entered her office. The desk was still bare in the center where Harris had made love to her. She shivered and looked away from it. Reaching at the same time for the handset of her phone.

"This is Sarah Malcolm," she said.

"It's Harris."

Her stomach dropped and her knees were weak. She sank into her office chair and looked at the Monet print on the wall. It was a walkway under snow. The

Impressionist brush strokes took the harsh reality off what was an Industrial town. She wished for a moment that someone could come into her life and paint her with those same strokes.

"Sarah?"

She wasn't ready to talk to him. Only by keeping busy for the last hour had she been able to put him from her mind. Her hand started to shake and she realized she wasn't ready for this. She might never be ready to talk to him again.

All she'd accomplished with her life had disappeared. And she was back at square one. With no experience or knowledge to help her through the situation. But she'd had twelve years experience, she reminded herself.

"Sarah? Are you there?"

She let out the breath she'd been holding and closed her eyes. "Yes."

"Talk to me," he said.

She wished she could. But her gut said conversation wasn't ever going to change Harris's mind. She realized that losing the restaurant hurt, but not as badly as being betrayed by Harris. How could she have been so naive as to not to see the real Harris. "I'm trying to think of something to say to you."

"Would calling me a bastard help?" he asked.

She was stunned at first but then chuckled. Maybe she hadn't been the blind one after all. She knew Harris had a hard time seeing himself as a lasting part of anything. Even companies. He helped them and moved on. "Maybe."

Silence echoed for a few moments and then she heard him sigh. "You're important to me. What can I do to make this right?"

"I wish I knew."

"How about if I buy you another building? You can start from scratch there. Maybe with the bakery you'd been thinking of adding to the restaurant."

"Why would you do that?" she asked, a twinge of hope spreading through her. He was going to confess his emotions for her. She might lose Taste of Home but she'd be okay with Harris by her side.

She'd known deep in her heart that he was capable of deep love for her. He just didn't know how to recognize it. But faced with losing each other seemed to have made him realize it. Or was she just hoping it did. Because Harris was the kind of man she wanted with her for the long haul. The kind of relationship that would last a lifetime. The kind of forever that she'd dreamed of since she first realized the differences between men and women.

"Because I want to make this right," Harris said. She knew he did. She could feel the force of his will through the phone.

A spark of hope sprung to life inside her and she had the first flash that maybe things weren't going to be as bad as she feared. Maybe this time she wasn't going to be alone. Maybe this time she'd loved wisely.

"Only one thing can make this right," she said, hoping she wouldn't have to say anything more.

"I've never had a relationship that lasted more than a few weeks."

"I know," she said. And she did know that. Even if he hadn't told her it was apparent in the way he was careful not to let anyone get to close too him.

"I want to make things right," he said again.

Disappointment swamped her. This time it hurt so much worse than before, because she'd hoped that he was calling with the seeds of the future. Instead she'd just realized that he wanted things to go on as they had been.

"Tell what it is and I'll do it, honey," he said.

She rubbed her eyes to keep from crying and took a deep breath before she said, "If I have to tell you then it will never work."

"I mean it, Sarah. No price is too high," he said.

"I think the price is too high, Harris. Because the only thing that could make this right is love."

"Love?"

"Yes, love. But you can't admit you feel anything for me, can you?"

"There has to be something else you want," he said.

"There isn't."

"How can you be sure that love will make this better? Honestly, I've seen some gruesome things done in the name of love."

"And I've seen miraculous things done by love."

He sighed heavily. "I guess this is goodbye then."

"I'd never have figured you for a coward, Harris."

"I'm not," he said.

"Yes, you are. When are you going to let go of the past and take a chance on the future?"

"I can't."

"Then you're not the man I thought you were."

"Who am I?"

"Just another guy I should have known better than to waste my time on," she said, slamming down the phone.

Harris packed his clothes quietly. The staff would come in later to box up his books and ship them along with his other household items to his home in Belair. Thinking about his home didn't bring the gratifying feeling he was used to.

The house had a garden that made Eden look like a child's first attempt at horticulture. His staff kept the place spotless and knew their places. They didn't ask him questions about his love life or interfere like Ray did. He should be excited to be going home. But instead he felt...empty.

Why?

He glanced around the hotel room and realized these last few weeks in Orlando had given him something he'd never had before. Something he'd never realized had been missing until Sarah. He glanced once again around the room and saw her ghost everywhere. Saw the couch where she'd waited for him in the dark. Only the fireworks lighting the room.

Saw the bookshelves crammed with titles they'd discussed. Saw the door to the bedroom—the threshold he'd carried her across before making her his.

He'd never been as close to another person as he had to Sarah.

He glanced around the room one more time while he walked toward the door. A new emotion kindled to life deep inside of him and he realized he missed Sarah.

But not enough to open his heart to the love she was sure he'd developed for her. He knew better. It didn't make sense but he was certain that love wasn't for him. He'd never confessed his love to another human. Not even his father. But then his father wasn't usually interested in anything or anyone who existed outside the penthouse.

Was that a fair judgment? He picked up his cell phone before he could think about it and dialed his dad's number. Felix, his father's butler, answered on the third ring.

"It's Harris. May I speak with my father?"

"He's under the weather, sir. Not taking any calls."

Harris started to hang up and stopped. But he needed to talk to his father. He'd never forced the issue before. "I, uh, I really need to talk to him, Felix."

"Yes, sir. I'll see if he'll take the call."

He heard Felix's footsteps and imagined the path the butler was taking. Through the marble-floored hallway up the carpeted stairs and then he heard Felix knock on the door. His father's rusty bid for Felix to enter. Was this his own future without Sarah?

He realized his perception of the parental role had

changed because of Sarah. She was always available for the twins. If she were in the hospital she'd take a call from them. She always put everyone she cared for before herself.

Had she done that for him? Would he really want her to? Someone should put Sarah first. Not someone, he realized. He should put Sarah first.

"Your son, sir, is on the phone," Felix said.

"I'm not taking calls today," his dad said.

So much for fatherly advice, Harris thought. "He said it was urgent," Felix said.

"Urgent?" his dad asked.

Harris heard a twinge of emotion in his father's voice. Not the same dull tone he'd been using earlier. Maybe he'd waited too long to call his dad.

"Yes, sir."

"I'll take it. Please open the curtains on your way out."

Opening the curtains was a big deal for his dad. When he wasn't depressed he spent his days on the rooftop garden, cultivating his roses and basking in the sun. But once his depression hit he'd lock himself away from the sun.

"Harris?" his father said. His dad, for all his weaknesses, had always been there for him and Harris felt a rush of emotion toward him.

"Dad, I'm sorry to disturb you."

"What can I do for you?" he asked.

The million-dollar question and he didn't know how to ask it. How was he going to ask his father why he hid away? How was he going to find out if the same thing that was inside his dad was inside him? How was he going to find the answers when he wasn't sure of the questions?

"Why did Mom leave?" Harris asked at last. When he thought about why he had troubles committing to women, the path always led back to that night he hated to remember.

His father sighed and Harris thought he might not answer him. "I wish I knew."

"Have you ever thought about that day?" Harris asked. They'd never spoken of his mom after she left and Harris had never really understood why. He remembered very little of her departure.

"It's all I do. Day after day."

"Dad, you need to get out. Go tend your roses or something outside," Harris said.

"Not today. Will you be on the East Coast anytime soon?"

"No," Harris said, the lie coming easily to him. He didn't want to visit his father. Especially with the holidays looming. He avoided the East Coast and his father's home. It made him uncomfortable and for the first time he realized why. There was a bit of the future in viewing his father locked away from the world alone.

Now he had another reason to stay away from the East Coast—Sarah. He didn't think he'd take any more jobs that weren't in Asia.

"Thanks for talking to me," Harris said. He didn't feel any closer to the answers he sought then he had before he'd called his dad.

"Harris…"

"Yes?"

"I know I've never been father of the year. But if you need me…I'm here."

"I know, Dad."

"I'm always here," his father said. The words had the sound of litany. One Harris had heard over and over when he'd been a child.

Harris hung up, convinced that the Davidson curse had struck again.

Eleven

Harris packed his bags methodically, telling himself this was no different than the hundred times he'd moved on in the past. But there was emptiness deep inside him. It wasn't new he realized. This was just the first time he'd been aware it was there.

He called down to make sure Ray was waiting out front and left the room, a suitcase in each hand. He knew that the memories he had of his time with Sarah would haunt him and for a short time, he was willing to let them.

He didn't want to forget her yet. In time they'd fade as all memories did and he'd be living once again in the cold gray area that he was most used to.

Ray opened the back door to the limo and reached for the bags to stow them. Harris sank back in the leather seat. The scent of Sarah's perfume lingered in the air. Was it only this morning that everything in his life seemed to finally be coming together?

How quickly the tide had changed. He rubbed the bridge of his nose feeling a headache coming on. Harris cursed under his breath.

"Where to, *compare?*" Ray asked from the front.

"The airport."

Ray frowned back at him. "You're leaving?"

Harris still didn't like the familiarity that Ray had with him. There should be no questions. Ray should take orders and that's the end of it. But Harris had come to like the rotund little man. He might actually miss the funny guy with his Italian cursing and bizarre phone conversations. "There's no reason for me to stay."

"Didn't you talk to Sarah?" Ray asked.

He wasn't going to share with anyone else the details of that conversation that made him feel like he'd come close to keeping her. And then a second later lost her for good. He'd never really understood what women needed from him. His mother had needed space—distance. His stepmoms had needed him to be invisible. Sarah needed love. The one thing he couldn't buy her.

He rubbed the back of his neck. Damn, this headache was going to be one hell of one. But physical weakness was one he didn't tolerate so he ignored the pain.

"There's no changing her mind."

"Did you send her a gift?"

"It's useless. She wants something from me I can't give her."

"What?"

"Love."

"Ah, *amore.* Why can't you give it to her?"

"It's like trying to get water from a stone. I don't have anything to give," Harris said, not sure why he was telling this to Ray. Maybe because he hadn't been able to get anything from his dad.

"What made you a stone?" Ray asked.

Harris didn't answer. He only knew he'd always known caring was a liability and that loving someone was a risk that wasn't worth taking. He wished he remembered more of the day his mother had left them.

"Why don't we go have a drink? I'll help you come up with a plan."

"Ray, there's nothing you could do to change my mind."

"*Merda.* Make sure your seat belt is tight."

"Why?"

"I'm going to change your mind."

The car moved away from the Dolphin but instead of heading toward the lights of I-4 and the airport Ray drove toward the darkened landscape that was undeveloped property, continuing to pick up speed. Going faster and faster.

"I don't scare easily."

Images flashed past the windows to fast for Harris to identify them. He sank deeper into the seat and wondered if maybe this wasn't a pain-induced delusion.

Finally the car slowed and pulled to a stop. Harris was definitely calling the limo company tomorrow and having Ray fired. The guy had slipped over the edge.

"Where are we?" Harris asked.

"Unless I've lost my touch, 1978 Connecticut."

Clearly, Ray was psycho. Harris didn't know if it would be better to pretend to buy into his illusion if he should be the voice of reason and try to talk Ray down.

"Why are you doing this? Do you feel okay?" Harris asked.

"I wish it were only *agita*. I was assigned to be your driver to make sure you and Sarah fell in love."

"Who assigned you to do that?" Harris asked, humoring the driver.

"A smart-ass angel."

Harris wondered if Ray didn't have a split personality disorder. He'd seemed so sane prior to this.

"You've got to be kidding."

"I wish."

"How'd that happen?" Harris asked.

"When I was killed I asked God for forgiveness."

"And he said, sure, just make Harris Davidson fall in love. I'm not buying it."

Ray was suddenly by Harris's side. He didn't see the man move but there he was. He leaned into Harris personal space, in a clearly intimidating manner. Maybe he should just say he'd see Sarah again.

"Just shut up and listen. I'm buying my way to heaven one heart at a time."

"I know you believe what you're saying—"

"*Merda,* I sound like a *gavone,* but this is true."

Harris said nothing.

"Enough talking. Follow me."

Harris wasn't getting out of the car with a crazy man who claimed he was a dead matchmaker that could travel back in time.

But Ray grabbed his arm and Harris found himself standing on the portico in front of his childhood home. Floodlights illuminating the topiaries in the front yard. The big brick fortress that he'd spent the first six years of his life in.

Harris realized he was buying into Ray's delusion. He closed his eyes and reopened them but the house remained. What year had Ray said? God, don't let this be real, he thought. Because if it was he was going to have to remember something he'd spent a lifetime trying to forget.

"Let's go inside."

Harris stepped away from Ray and leaned against the limo. "I'll wait here."

"This whole trip is for you."

Ray grabbed Harris's arm and this time snapped his fingers. They flew up the side of the building into a room that Harris hadn't been in since he was six. It was the master bedroom. Every light blazed in the room. Felix, his dad's butler, and Mary, Felix's wife, stood anxiously by the open door. Harris refused to look at the bed. He knew what he'd see. Didn't want to see it.

Because suddenly he remembered the day his mother left. It all came rushing back and he knew why he'd spent a lifetime keeping other people at bay.

"What's the point in this?" Harris asked.

"You picked this moment in time."

He glanced at the bed piled high with suitcases. Slowly panned over to his father. A much younger version of his father stood stoically next to the window. Harris saw himself. A six-year-old boy clinging to his father's hand.

God, he looked so scared. He didn't like looking that way. It seemed to Harris that all those emotions should have been inside so that no one would know how bad he'd felt. He didn't want pity, even then.

He glanced around the room at the other players in his mother's little drama and saw Felix watching him with…damn pity. "What's the point in this?"

"Just watch," Ray said.

But Harris didn't want to. He didn't understand why reliving the night he and his father had begged *her* to stay was going to help with anything. But his father wasn't saying anything. The boy did all the taking.

"Mommy, where are you going?"

She tossed a rainbow of silk dresses into a suitcase without care. Her attention clearly on one objective. Getting out has quickly as possible. "Away."

"Why?"

"You're a big boy now, Harris. You started school

today. You don't need me,'' she said. His mother was a beautiful woman. Harris knew what the boy was going to say next and didn't want to watch it.

"Let's go, Ray."

"Not yet," Ray said, keeping his eyes on the mother and son discussion.

"I need you, Mommy."

"Dammit, kid, you're just like your father…too needy. I can't give you anything more."

Harris watched his father stroke his head and remembered how strong his dad had been that day. That one day. "Mary, take Harris to his room."

Mary moved forward to take his hand but Harris knew his six-year-old self wouldn't give up that easily. "I love you, Mommy."

She looked at him, her eyes the same pretty green as the emerald necklace his father had given her at Christmas. "Love is a weakness, Harris."

Ray took his arm and Harris found himself back in the car sitting in front of the Dolphin. Had he just dreamed the entire episode?

"Ray?"

"Yes, sir?" Ray said.

"Did we just…?" Harris wasn't going to say anything else. He didn't want to sound insane. But everything had seemed so real. He remembered the rest of that night. How he'd vowed to never fall in love. To never say he loved another person again. It was time to let go of that vow.

Sarah wasn't having the best day. Her car was acting up again, the twins were fighting and Roger had taken a job as a manager at the Olive Garden on Sand Lake Road. All in all her life had definitely gone down hill in the last three days. Thanksgiving was in two days. Taste of Home was being evicted in four days.

She hadn't slept since Harris had left. Since their last conversation, which somehow hadn't felt right. Maybe she should have settled for what he could give. But she wasn't short-changing herself anymore. Once she'd let him buy his way back into her good graces their relationship would change. And she'd never wanted Harris for his money.

She'd wanted him for his lonely heart, which he guarded so closely. And for his dry wit, which he wielded like a shield until she'd gotten close enough that he'd started to trust her. And for his keen intelligence.

But he hadn't offered her those things. And she hadn't been brave enough to ask him for them. The one other time she'd asked a man to stay—Paul—he'd left.

For the first time since she'd turned eighteen she had no idea what to do next. Today would be the last night that the restaurant was open. She walked through the empty tables they didn't open for two more hours. Soon the chefs would arrive to start cooking and then the wait-staff would be here. But for now it was just Sarah. She'd have to pick up the slack since Roger had bailed.

She glanced at the small dance floor remembered

the first time Harris had taken her in his arms out there. Remembered the pulsing beat of the mambo and the heat that still burned inside her for him.

The register where Burt had teased Harris about dancing. And Harris had looked at her with his North Atlantic eyes and made her feel like the sexiest woman on the earth.

The kitchen refrigerator where she'd stowed the flowers he'd given her. Her office where he'd made love to her. And where he'd hidden from her on her Halloween.

Finally she turned toward her dad's office, opening the door. Burt and Isabella were going to pack the office up this afternoon. Sarah went to her father's big leather chair and sat in it. It still smelled faintly of the cigars her dad used to smoke. Her mom's picture was on the edge of the desk. Her parents love surrounded her.

"What am I going to do?" she asked her mom's portrait.

"Follow your heart." At first she'd thought her mom was talking to her but then she realized the voice had come from the doorway.

Ray King was standing there. "What are you doing here?" she asked.

Ray entered the room. She liked the man. He was friendly and funny. And there was a warm kindness in his eyes that she'd never really noticed before.

"Trying to help you," he said. "Harris asked me to come pick you up."

Sarah was beginning to feel mean. Harris had sent

flowers and candy. A large basket of cooking supplies and a bear wearing a chef's hat. And last night a book of Byron poetry and a new jazz CD. He was showering her with gifts but she was afraid to take them. Afraid if she did then she'd take whatever he had to give her no matter the cost to herself.

So she'd sent the gifts back.

"I'm not ready to talk to him. But I appreciate your stopping by."

"So are you going to follow my advice?" he asked.

Follow her heart. "I've tried. Did you know this was my dad's office?"

Ray glanced around the room. She wondered what he thought of the dark decor and the layer of dust. "Your old man's dead?"

"My mom, too. This place is all I have left of them." She couldn't really explain it but this was the last place she had that they'd walked and she didn't want to lose it. She wanted to be able to come into this room and thanks to New Deal Developers and Harris Davidson she couldn't. She'd talked to them and they weren't budging. They wanted her out.

Her business had been in trouble long before Harris came on the scene. Long before The New Deal Developers had looked at this strip mall and decided to revamp it. Long before she'd fallen in love with him and wished for a different ending to their story.

She stopped blaming Harris for not telling her the same evening she'd learned of the eviction. Once she'd calmed down she realized that business was just that—business. She knew she'd leaped on the restaurant as a way to test Harris. And it was test neither of them passed.

"The past is always hard to leave behind. But this place isn't the only memory you have of your parents," Ray said.

Sarah realized he was right. Her memories weren't going to disappear just because she didn't own this restaurant. She carried them inside her and always would. "Who'd you leave behind?"

"No one. I didn't let any one person close enough…."

Was this her future—someone who kept everyone at bay because she knew how much it hurt to love? She reached out and took Ray's hand in hers. "I'm sorry."

"Don't be. I made my choices. I can live with my regrets. Can you?" he asked. He turned her hand over in his offering comfort in return.

She wasn't ready to talk about that now. "I know what you're trying to say. I don't regret my actions."

"Not now when the fire of anger is still burning inside of you but in time you will."

"He betrayed me, Ray. He knew my business was going to be shut down and he didn't tell me."

"Is that really why you're mad?" Ray asked, pointedly.

She thought about it for a few moments. She knew it wasn't but she felt too vulnerable to say otherwise. She didn't like being this fragile. Not being sure of her future. Professionally or personally. Though she'd been offered a job as manager from a chain restaurant on International Drive. So at least she and the twins weren't going to starve. But she didn't know if she could work for someone else. "I'm not sure."

"You have to be honest with yourself before you can expect honesty from others."

"That sounds like a quote. I've always been honest with myself."

"Then you shouldn't have any problems, eh?" he said.

"What do you want from me?" she asked.

"Fulfill your parents' dream."

"The restaurant?" she asked, afraid to acknowledge the truth.

He tipped his head to one side. "Now where's the honesty?"

Ray walked away. Sarah sank back in her father's chair and took a good hard look at herself and her life. Realizing that she hadn't been living her dreams but her parents. And that her dreams involved Harris.

"Ray, wait. I'm ready to go and see Harris."

Twelve

Harris was nervous. It wasn't a pleasant sensation and he'd tried to analyze why he was so anxious but the answers he'd received hadn't pleased him. It was never a good policy to allow emotion into a decision matrix. His mind said that this building and the plans he'd made for a new restaurant were enough to win Sarah back. But his gut disagreed.

This was his last ditch effort. He'd pulled out all the stops and spent an insane amount of money to make everything as close to perfect as he could get it.

Still his hands were sweaty and his pulse was racing. Never had the outcome of any business deal meant so much to him. He ran a finger under his collar. Then straightened his tie. Glancing around the empty room he saw what he hoped was the future.

On Monday the table and chairs he'd ordered would be delivered. On Tuesday the decor from Taste of Home would be transferred and hung on the walls. On Wednesday unless everything went to hell, the new restaurant would have a soft opening for just family and friends.

But today there was only one table with a lit candle on it. Dinner, which he'd picked up from a Thai restaurant on his way over, and a boom box CD player near the dance floor.

The location was in downtown Orlando in the newly revitalized section of Thornton Park. Close by were family neighborhoods and trendy new condos. As soon as Sarah had sent the first gift back he'd realized simple presents weren't going to be enough. So he'd scouted locations and finally found this one. The building was now his and he had the deed to give to Sarah.

He hoped this would make amends in her mind. But he knew that it wasn't his conscience forcing him to act but his heart. He wanted things to be right in her world so that he could convince her to give him another chance. Convince her somehow that loving him wasn't a mistake. Convince her that he could be her forever man.

The door opened and Harris turned. Sarah stood unsure in the doorway. The Florida weather was a little nippy this evening and she wore a light coat.

"Hello, Harris," she said. She was back lit from

the street light and the glow around her made her seem ethereal. He'd never felt more mortal. His feet so strongly clay and his body so easily given to mistakes.

"Hi," he said. Wow, you could tell he was a man corporations relied on for his keen observations. Why could this one woman turn him to a stuttering idiot?

"Ray said you wanted to see me," she said.

"I do. Thanks for coming," he said. He crossed the empty room to her side.

"You're welcome," she said.

She smelled just like his memories. Faintly floral and all woman. His body took notice. His blood flowing heavier in his veins. His skin tightening and his hands tingling with the need to touch her.

He knew right then that if the restaurant didn't work then he'd resort to what his instincts said would work. Taking her in his arms and making love to her until he'd erased all the doubts about him from her mind.

She stared up at him. Her chocolaty-brown eyes wide with emotion. He reached for her and she tensed. This wasn't going to be easy, he thought.

He took her coat and tossed it over the bar. He led her to the table and pulled out a chair for her. She watched him wearily. He had no idea how to reassure her.

"Wine?"

She nodded. He poured her a glass of Merlot. He'd planned every detail and everything was as perfect as it could be. But suddenly perfection didn't seem enough.

He seated himself and lifted his glass to her for a toast. "To the future."

Her gaze never left his. She set her glass on the table without taking a sip. "I'm not sure why I'm here. What is this place?"

"Your new location for Taste of Home."

"Why?"

"I've thought about what you said...."

"And?"

"I wanted to replace what I'd taken from you. I want to return everything to where it was so we can continue to move forward."

"I can't," she said.

Damn, he felt her slipping away. He was powerless to do anything to stop her. He realized he wasn't going to get to keep her.

"Why not? This is a great location. There are family neighborhoods nearby as well as being close to downtown for the lunch crowds. That's the perfect clientele for your restaurant. I haven't had time to do an in-depth study but I'm planning—"

"Harris," she said.

Just his name, but with so much emotion he felt his plans slide away. Sarah had wised up and knew that a shell of a man wasn't for her. That no matter how much love she poured into him, nothing was going to come back.

But she was wrong. He had a deep well of emotion

waiting for her. Could he take the risk of letting her see it?

"I don't want you to buy your way back to me."

"I was afraid of that," he said.

She pushed her chair back and started toward the door. "No man has ever made such a big gesture for me," she said over her shoulder.

"Good," he said.

She pivoted.

Harris felt light-headed and weak but he walked to where she stood. He took her shoulders in his hands and lifted her into his body. Lowering his head he took her mouth in a deep kiss. There was nothing tentative in it because he'd realized that bold measures were needed. And he drew strength from this woman who'd come to mean the world to him.

He lifted his head, pleased to see that her eyes were dazed and her face flushed.

"I have one more thing to say to you."

She bit her bottom lip and he noticed the sheen of tears in her eyes.

"I…" Oh, God, he couldn't say the words. He felt like he was six again and he didn't think he could do it.

He started to let his hands drop to his sides, but he caught his hands and she leaned up brushing her lips against his neck.

"You…?" she asked. He saw hope shining in her eyes and he realized that when two people loved each other there was no vulnerability.

He leaned down and whispered the words in her ear. "I love you."

She laughed and hugged him tightly to her. "I love you, too."

"Still?" he asked. Damn, did he have to sound so needy.

"Even when I was so mad at you for being stubborn, I still loved you."

"I'm new to this."

"I am, too," she said.

He bent his head, taking her mouth with his again. He reached into his pocket and pulled out the small box, he'd optimistically put there earlier. The one he hadn't let himself think about until he had her in his arms.

He slid to his knees in front of her. "I have a question."

She dropped to her knees next to him. But he didn't want her there with him. He wanted her to understand that he was hers. That she humbled him in ways he'd never known he could be humbled and he wanted to be better for her.

"Will you marry me?" he asked.

"Yes," she said, throwing herself into his arms again. He lost his balance and fell backward. She was sprawled on top of him.

He slipped the ring on her finger and kissed the palm of her hand. "Don't ever stop loving me."

"I won't."

"Even if I make you mad."

"Even then."

He got them both to their feet. He wanted to make love to her but knew her siblings were coming by. He'd invited them to join he and Sarah for dessert. At the time he'd been hoping they'd have good news and it turned out he was right.

He'd invited Ray as well. Thirty minutes later, Harris was relieved to find that all the Malcolms were pleased with his engagement to Sarah. They sat around the table and talked about plans for the future and for the first time ever, Harris felt apart of something permanent and lasting. And he knew he'd found the home he'd been searching for a long time.

Epilogue

"Well, well, Pasquale, you did okay," said a voice from behind me.

"Hey, babe. That's Il Re to you," I said, turning to see the angel broad.

"What'd I say about calling me babe?" she asked.

I smiled realizing I felt pretty good. For a minute I wished Tess could see me. Of course, she couldn't, but I knew this was a job she'd be proud I'd done. "Can't help it, I'm wallowing in victory."

"Don't wallow too long."

"Why not?"

"Because strictly speaking you didn't do things exactly by the book."

He raised one eyebrow at her. "You didn't give

me a book. All you said was they had to be married
And Il Re delivered.''

"I'll give you that. I thought we'd talked about you
being the king," she said.

"I just realized that I could still be the king," I
said.

"Oh, yeah?"

"Yeah, the king of hearts."

She almost smiled. I saw her lips twitched. But she
vanished and I was standing alone outside the church
where Harris and Sarah were getting married. I was
glad they'd made it. Glad I'd done something to make
the world a better place.

Merda, I was sounding like a gavone. But it didn't
bother me. I didn't have any *compares* to see me any
more. Just my conscience to keep me company. And
my conscience said being the king of hearts was the
right title for me.

*   *   *   *   *

Turn the page for a bonus look at the next title in Katherine Garbera's
KING OF HEARTS *miniseries:*

CINDERELLA'S CHRISTMAS AFFAIR

by Katherine Garbera
November 2003

One

Of course the first man she'd had a crush on would be the only thing standing between her and her promotion. C. J. Terrence smiled with a confidence she was far from feeling and shook Tad Randolph's hand.

Ten years had passed since they'd last seen each other and she knew she'd changed a lot. She'd dyed her mousy-brown hair a sassy auburn, she'd swapped her horn-rimmed glasses for aqua colored contacts that masked her natural brown color. And the biggest thing of all she'd lost twenty pounds.

But in that moment she felt like the chubby girl next door. She reached for the bridge of her nose to push up the glasses she'd always wore back then. Dropping her hand, she reminded herself that she'd changed.

She took a deep breath; assured herself that her physical changes were enough to keep Tad from recognizing her. Of course, she recognized him and he'd put on at least twenty pounds. All of it solid muscle. He was exactly how she'd expect the owner of a sporting goods company to look.

It was too bad he couldn't be balding like other guys who were his age. Instead his blond hair was thick as ever and bleached by the sun. He looked too good and she wanted to leave immediately.

''C. J. Terrence,'' she said introducing herself. She could only hope that maybe Tad wouldn't be able to place her and identify her as the girl he'd known as Cathy Jane in high school.

*   *   *   *   *

If you enjoyed what you just read,
then we've got an offer you can't resist!

Take 2 bestselling love stories FREE!

Plus get a FREE surprise gift!

Your opinion is important to us! Please take a few moments to share your thoughts with us about your experiences with Harlequin and Silhouette books. Your comments will be very useful in ensuring that we deliver books you love to read.
Please take a few minutes to complete the questionnaire, then send it to us at the address below.

Send your completed questionnaires to:
Harlequin/Silhouette Reader Survey, P.O. Box 9046, Buffalo, NY 14269-9046

1. As you may know, there are many different lines under the Harlequin and Silhouette brands. Each of the lines is listed below. Please check the box that most represents your reading habit for each line.

Line	Currently read this line	Do not read this line	Not sure if I read this line
Harlequin American Romance	❏	❏	❏
Harlequin Duets	❏	❏	❏
Harlequin Romance	❏	❏	❏
Harlequin Historicals	❏	❏	❏
Harlequin Superromance	❏	❏	❏
Harlequin Intrigue	❏	❏	❏
Harlequin Presents	❏	❏	❏
Harlequin Temptation	❏	❏	❏
Harlequin Blaze	❏	❏	❏
Silhouette Special Edition	❏	❏	❏
Silhouette Romance	❏	❏	❏
Silhouette Intimate Moments	❏	❏	❏
Silhouette Desire	❏	❏	❏

2. Which of the following best describes why you bought *this book?* One answer only, please.

the picture on the cover	❏	the title	❏
the author	❏	the line is one I read often	❏
part of a miniseries	❏	saw an ad in another book	❏
saw an ad in a magazine/newsletter	❏	a friend told me about it	❏
I borrowed/was given this book	❏	other: _____	❏

3. Where did you buy *this book?* One answer only, please.

at Barnes & Noble	❏	at a grocery store	❏
at Waldenbooks	❏	at a drugstore	❏
at Borders	❏	on eHarlequin.com Web site	❏
at another bookstore	❏	from another Web site	❏
at Wal-Mart	❏	Harlequin/Silhouette Reader	❏
at Target	❏	Service/through the mail	
at Kmart	❏	used books from anywhere	❏
at another department store or mass merchandiser	❏	I borrowed/was given this book	❏

4. On average, how many Harlequin and Silhouette books do you buy at one time?

I buy _____ books at one time	❏
I rarely buy a book	❏

MRQ403SD-1A

5. How many times per month do you shop for any *Harlequin and/or Silhouette* books?
   One answer only, please.

1 or more times a week	❑	a few times per year	❑
1 to 3 times per month	❑	less often than once a year	❑
1 to 2 times every 3 months	❑	never	❑

6. When you think of your ideal heroine, which *one* statement describes her the best?
   One answer only, please.

She's a woman who is strong-willed		She's a desirable woman	❑
She's a woman who is needed by others	❑	She's a powerful woman	❑
She's a woman who is taken care of		She's a passionate woman	❑
She's an adventurous woman		She's a sensitive woman	❑

7. The following statements describe types or genres of books that you may be
   interested in reading. Pick *up to 2 types* of books that you are most interested in.

I like to read about truly romantic relationships	❑
I like to read stories that are sexy romances	❑
I like to read romantic comedies	❑
I like to read a romantic mystery/suspense	❑
I like to read about romantic adventures	❑
I like to read romance stories that involve family	❑
I like to read about a romance in times or places that I have never seen	❑
Other: _____	❑

*The following questions help us to group your answers with those readers who are
similar to you. Your answers will remain confidential.*

8. Please record your year of birth below.
   19 _____

9. What is your marital status?
   single ❑   married ❑   common-law ❑   widowed ❑
   divorced/separated ❑

10. Do you have children 18 years of age or younger currently living at home?
    yes ❑   no ❑

11. Which of the following best describes your employment status?
    employed full-time or part-time ❑   homemaker ❑   student ❑
    retired ❑   unemployed ❑

12. Do you have access to the Internet from either home or work?
    yes ❑   no ❑

13. Have you ever visited eHarlequin.com?
    yes ❑   no ❑

14. What state do you live in?
    _____

15. Are you a member of Harlequin/Silhouette Reader Service?
    yes ❑   Account # _____   no ❑   MRQ403SD-1B

Is your man too good to be true?

Hot, gorgeous AND romantic?
If so, he could be a Harlequin® Blaze™ series cover model!

Our grand-prize winners will receive a trip for two to New York City to
shoot the cover of a Blaze novel, and will stay at the luxurious Plaza Hotel.
Plus, they'll receive $500 U.S. spending money!
The runner-up winners will receive $200 U.S.
to spend on a romantic dinner for two.

It's easy to enter!

In 100 words or less, tell us what makes your boyfriend or spouse a true romantic
and the perfect candidate for the cover of a Blaze novel, and include in your submission
two photos of this potential cover model.

All entries must include the written submission of the contest entrant, two photographs of the model
candidate and the Official Entry Form and Publicity Release forms completed in full and signed by
both the model candidate and the contest entrant. Harlequin, along with the experts at
Elite Model Management, will select a winner.

For photo and complete Contest details, please refer to the Official Rules on the next page. All entries
will become the property of Harlequin Enterprises Ltd. and are not returnable.

**Please visit www.blazecovermodel.com to download a copy of the Official Entry Form and
Publicity Release Form or send a request to one of the addresses below.**

Please mail your entry to: **Harlequin Blaze Cover Model Search**

In U.S.A.
P.O. Box 9069
Buffalo, NY
14269-9069

In Canada
P.O. Box 637
Fort Erie, ON
L2A 5X3

No purchase necessary. Contest open to Canadian and U.S. residents who are 18 and over.
Void where prohibited. Contest closes September 30, 2003.

HBCVRMODEL1

HARLEQUIN BLAZE COVER MODEL SEARCH CONTEST 3569 OFFICIAL RULES
NO PURCHASE NECESSARY TO ENTER

1. To enter, submit two (2) 4" x 6" photographs of a boyfriend or spouse (who must be 18 years of age or older) taken no later than three (3) months from the time of entry: a close-up, waist up, shirtless photograph; and a fully clothed, full-length photograph, then, tell us, in 100 words or fewer, why he should be a Harlequin Blaze cover model and how he is romantic. Your complete "entry" must include: (i) your essay, (ii) the Official Entry Form and Publicity Release Form printed below completed and signed by you (as "Entrant"), (iii) the photographs (with your hand-written name, address and phone number, and your model's name, address and phone number on the back of each photograph), and (iv) the Publicity Release Form and Photograph Representation Form printed below completed and signed by your model (as "Model"), and should be sent via first-class mail to either: Harlequin Blaze Cover Model Search Contest 3569, P.O. Box 9069, Buffalo, NY, 14269-9069, or Harlequin Blaze Cover Model Search Contest 3569, P.O. Box 637, Fort Erie, Ontario L2A 5X3. All submissions must be in English and be received no later than September 30, 2003. Limit: one entry per person, household or organization. **Purchase or acceptance of a product offer does not improve your chances of winning.** All entry requirements must be strictly adhered to for eligibility and to ensure fairness among entries.

2. Ten (10) Finalist submissions (photographs and essays) will be selected by a panel of judges consisting of members of the Harlequin editorial, marketing and public relations staff, as well as a representative from Elite Model Management (Toronto) Inc., based on the following criteria:

Aptness/Appropriateness of submitted photographs for a Harlequin Blaze cover—70%
Originality of Essay—20%
Sincerity of Essay—10%

In the event of a tie, duplicate finalists will be selected. The photographs submitted by finalists will be posted on the Harlequin website no later than November 15, 2003 (at www.blazecovermodel.com), and viewers may vote, in rank order, on their favorite(s) to assist in the panel of judges' final determination of the Grand Prize and Runner-up winning entries based on the above judging criteria. All decisions of the judges are final.

3. All entries become the property of Harlequin Enterprises Ltd. and none will be returned. Any entry may be used for future promotional purposes. Elite Model Management (Toronto) Inc. or its partners, subsidiaries and affiliates operating as "Elite Model Management" will have access to all entries including all personal information, and may contact any Entrant and/or Model in its sole discretion for their own business purposes. Harlequin and Elite Model Management (Toronto) Inc. are separate entities with no legal association or partnership whatsoever having no power to bind or obligate the other or create any expressed or implied obligation or responsibility on behalf of the other, such that Harlequin shall not be responsible in any way for any acts or omissions of Elite Model Management (Toronto) Inc. or its partners, subsidiaries and affiliates in connection with the Contest or otherwise and Elite Model Management shall not be responsible in any way for any acts or omissions of Harlequin or its partners, subsidiaries and affiliates in connection with the contest or otherwise.

4. All Entrants and Models must be residents of the U.S. or Canada, be 18 years of age or older, and have no prior criminal convictions. The contest is not open to any Model that is a professional model and/or actor in any capacity at the time of the entry. Contest void wherever prohibited by law; all applicable laws and regulations apply. Any litigation within the Province of Quebec regarding the conduct or organization of a publicity contest may be submitted to the Régie des alcools, des courses et des jeux for a ruling, and any litigation regarding the awarding of a prize may be submitted to the Régie only for the purpose of helping the parties reach a settlement. Employees and immediate family members of Harlequin Enterprises Ltd., D.L. Blair, Inc., Elite Model Management (Toronto) Inc. and their parents, affiliates, subsidiaries and all other agencies, entities and persons connected with the use, marketing or conduct of this Contest are not eligible to enter. Acceptance of any prize offered constitutes permission to use Entrants' and Models' names, essay submissions, photographs or other likenesses for the purposes of advertising, trade, publication and promotion on behalf of Harlequin Enterprises Ltd., its parent, affiliates, subsidiaries, assigns and other authorized entities involved in the judging and promotion of the contest without further compensation to any Entrant or Model, unless prohibited by law.

5. Finalists will be determined no later than October 30, 2003. Prize Winners will be determined no later than January 31, 2004. Grand Prize Winners (consisting of winning Entrant and Model) will be required to sign and return Affidavit of Eligibility/Release of Liability and Model Release forms within thirty (30) days of notification. Non-compliance with this requirement and within the specified time period will result in disqualification and an alternate will be selected. Any prize notification returned as undeliverable will result in the awarding of the prize to an alternate set of winners. All travelers (or parent/legal guardian of a minor) must execute the Affidavit of Eligibility/Release of Liability prior to ticketing and must possess required travel documents (e.g. valid photo ID) where applicable. Travel dates specified by Sponsor but no later than May 30, 2004.

6. Prizes: One (1) Grand Prize—the opportunity for the Model to appear on the cover of a paperback book from the Harlequin Blaze series, and a 3 day/2 night trip for two (Entrant and Model) to New York, NY for the photo shoot of Model which includes round-trip coach air transportation from the commercial airport nearest the winning Entrant's home to New York, NY, (or, in lieu of air transportation, $100 cash payable to Entrant and Model, if the winning Entrant's home is within 250 miles of New York, NY), hotel accommodations (double occupancy) at the Plaza Hotel and $500 cash spending money payable to Entrant and Model, (approximate prize value: $8,000), and one (1) Runner-up Prize of $200 cash payable to Entrant and Model for a romantic dinner for two (approximate prize value: $200). Prizes are valued in U.S. currency. Prizes consist of only those items listed as part of the prize. No substitution of prize(s) permitted by winners. All prizes are awarded jointly to the Entrant and Model of the winning entries, and are not severable - prizes and obligations may not be assigned or transferred. Any change to the Entrant and/or Model of the winning entries will result in disqualification and an alternate will be selected. Taxes on prize are the sole responsibility of winners. Any and all expenses and/or items not specifically described as part of the prize are the sole responsibility of winners. Harlequin Enterprises Ltd. and D.L. Blair, Inc., their parents, affiliates, and subsidiaries are not responsible for errors in printing of Contest entries and/or game pieces. No responsibility is assumed for lost, stolen, late, illegible, incomplete, inaccurate, non-delivered, postage due or misdirected mail or entries. In the event of printing or other errors which may result in unintended prize values or duplication of prizes, all affected game pieces or entries shall be null and void.

7. Winners will be notified by mail. For winners' list (available after March 31, 2004), send a self-addressed, stamped envelope to: Harlequin Blaze Cover Model Search Contest 3569 Winners, P.O. Box 4200, Blair, NE 68009-4200, or refer to the Harlequin website (at www.blazecovermodel.com).

Contest sponsored by Harlequin Enterprises Ltd., P.O. Box 9042, Buffalo, NY 14269-9042.

HBCVRMODEL2

COMING NEXT MONTH

#1537 MAN IN CONTROL—Diana Palmer
Long, Tall Texans
Undercover agent Alexander Cobb joined forces with his sworn
enemy Jodie Clayburn to crack a case. Surprisingly, working together
proved to be the easy part. The trouble they faced was fighting the
fiery attraction that threatened to consume them both!

#1538 BORN TO BE WILD—Anne Marie Winston
Dynasties: The Barones
Celia Papleo had been just a girl when Reese Barone sailed out of
her life, leaving her heart shattered. But now she was all woman—
and more than a match for the wealthy man who tempted her again.
Could a night of passion erase the misunderstandings of the past?

#1539 TEMPTING THE TYCOON—Cindy Gerard
Helping women find their happily-ever-afters was wedding planner
Rachel Matthew's trade. But she refused to risk her own heart. That
didn't stop roguishly charming millionaire lawyer Nate McGrory
from wanting to claim her for himself…and envisioning her icy
facade turing to molten lava at his touch!

#1540 LONETREE RANCHERS: MORGAN—Kathie DeNosky
Owning the most successful ranch in Wyoming was
Morgan Wakefield's dream. And it was now within his grasp—as
long as he wed Samantha Peterson. Their marriage was strictly a
business arrangement—but it didn't stem the desire they felt when
together….

#1541 HAVING THE BEST MAN'S BABY—Shawna Delacorte
For Jean Summerfield, the one thing worse than having to wear a
bridesmaid dress was facing her unreliable ex, best man Ry Collier.
But Jean's dormant desire sparked to life at Ry's touch. Would Ry
stay to face the consequences of their passion, or leave her burned
once more?

#1542 COWBOY'S MILLION-DOLLAR SECRET—
Emilie Rose
Charismatic cowboy Patrick Lander knew exactly who he was—
until virginal beauty Leanna Jensen brought news that Patrick
would inherit his biological father's multimillion-dollar estate! The
revelation threw Patrick's settled life into chaos—but paled compared
to the emotions Leanna aroused in him.

SDCNM0903